THE
CONVERSION
OF
RONNIE
VEE

Jenn,

All the best —

Love,

Michael

Also by Michael André Fath
Published by iUniverse

Novels
The Girls of Yesterday
The Village Squires – Tales of Mayhem and Revenge

Poetry
Reflections of Darkness and Light
Amor est Conceptualis
28 Benedizioni di Rita

Motivational
Faces Are Three of Virtuosity

THE CONVERSION OF RONNIE VEE

Michael André Fath

THE CONVERSION OF RONNIE VEE

iUniverse books may be ordered through booksellers or by contacting:

iUniverse
1663 Liberty Drive
Bloomington, IN 47403
www.iuniverse.com
1-800-Authors (1-800-288-4677)

ISBN: 978-1-5320-4542-4 (sc)
ISBN: 978-1-5320-4544-8 (hc)
ISBN: 978-1-5320-4543-1 (e)

Print information available on the last page.

iUniverse rev. date: 03/22/2018

THANKS TO

My daughters Jade and Sierra; my brother Vic and mom Elizabeth; il mio amore e compagno di lupo, Rita Conestabile; Rick Davis; Mike Waddell; Russell Anderson; Doc Keith Belote; Doc Millie Nandedkar; Doc Anne Ma; Stilson Greene; Linda Hayes; Stacy Carroll; Jim Spruell; Chris Neubauer and Corey Holland; Cerphe Colwell; Tommy McCarthy; Chris and Doug Grimes; Christian Scarborough; Prescott Engle; Tom Bateman; Steve Hartman; Mitch Herndon; my cousin Georgia; Steve Cummins; Eric Dean; Kate Reese; Jerry Curran; Patrick Thornton; Janet Gilman; Dan Derner; Doc Dunning; David Sharpe; Rhonda, Christine and Liz; my students and fans; and, my friends, who are too numerous to mention. **And very importantly, to all of those that have supported my literary adventures all these years...I am forever in your debt!**

I would also like to mention my high school principal James McBride, my high school football coach Ron Pyles, and guidance counselor Elizabeth Fath, whose real-life conviction in said responsibilities saved more than a few souls and inspired more than a few thoughts in this story.

Lastly, I thank God, once again!

CREDITS AND SPECIAL THANKS TO

Stilson Greene – Graphic Design
David Sharpe – Photography
Linda Hayes – Editing
Legal: Paice, Mougin-Boul, Smith

DEDICATION

This novel is most lovingly dedicated to Stilson Greene.

My life-long friend and supporter of my artistic endeavors
over the last 30 years, he has been with me throughout
all of the requisite pain and suffering that comes with
the precarious territory of touching those inner levels
of creativity...whether music, poetry or prose.
The brilliant novelist, Pat Conroy, once told me, "I lose
a piece of my soul every single time that I write."
After finishing this novel, I am yet again reminded
of Pat's prescient words of advice so many years ago,
and taken, then and now, literally, to heart.
Not only has Stilson conceptually envisioned my intentions,
but his philosophical reminders of life have helped me
survive the process. Plus, his friendship has greatly
contributed in saving me, more than a few times.
Thank you, my brother, I so love you...

Michael André Fath

THE CONVERSION OF RONNIE VEE

Many streams of consciousness
Forever emanating from thee
The plan, your plan, to save a soul
And to enlighten, spiritually

Our young, many possessed
Absence of inner-harmony
The words and belief, you express
Fate's cruel hand, now absentee

The white wolf, your brother
God's plan for you to see
A connection, marvelously profound
For both to run carefree

Alas, no one immune from suffering
Including your very own reality
Trust you gave, you'll need to find
And twist darkness into glee

Ronin Maximus Van Valkenburg
Youth handed you sobriquet, free
Myriad connections, all so beautiful
The Conversion of Ronnie Vee

I

He was enjoying the summer afternoon warmth and beauty of the brilliant Frankfurt sunshine, sitting on the edge of a typically ornate and quite majestic fountain, listening to its cascading water flow, just off of the Kaisserstrasse and not far from Die Club-Magie, where he had spent the previous evening in the company of two stunning Bavarian girls, sipping champagne and later culminating in a fairly spectacular finish back in his hotel suite, with single malt scotch, caviar and white chocolate being the consensus choice of all, at various intermissions, of course.

His inward smile brought him to reflect upon and appreciate his life, health and happiness, at least thus far.

Ronnie Van Valkenburg knew they were young, but not too, and well past those complicated and dangerous late-teenaged years and even beyond those precarious collegiate ones. His experience of counseling so many high school boys and girls had presented him a body of wisdom far beyond anything he had ever gleaned from the numerous years spent in pursuit of an undergraduate double major in psychology and philosophy, and later concluding with a very anti-climatic Ph.D. in Counseling.

Even his two years teaching at the collegiate level turned out to be an exercise in futility as many kids nowadays were so obviously and ridiculously entitled. Beginning with matriculation and then graduation, they all seemed to exactly have life figured out; where they were going to live, what career steps and status, how many kids, etc. Good fucking luck with that, he would often think. Plus, most university professors, especially in his field, were simply pompous assholes that he never could find the stomach to socialize with or even pretend to like, never mind respect.

Ronin Maximus Van Valkenburg was just as much an enigma as his given name; Dutch to be sure, but just enough reverence to the Japanese and Roman warriors his grandfather and father most vociferously studied and admired. As a kid, the sobriquets "Ronnie Vee" and later "V-V" and then simply "V" were implemented by his friends at such an early age that even his parents, two older sisters Vanessa and Valerie (which, as well, had presented each their own name challenge, to say the least) and close relatives ended up using each of these nicknames at various times.

He shut his eyes, letting the West German sun color his freshly shaved face, and was thinking about Lisa, a rising high school senior whose parents were divorcing and truly affecting her grades, demeanor and subsequent chances of getting into a good university.

She had slid into his office one afternoon, eyes filled with tears, just a few weeks ago, immediately after the final bell had tolled, ending that day's incarceration of the student body, as everyone was clearly counting the final days to summer break. Ronnie often mused at how each year nearly everyone at this particular time more or less just bailed on any kind of real application to study, and figured a way to slide by, still maintaining his or her own individual progress for the year. He also knew that this existence was a certain aspect of intelligence and it never failed to make him smile.

"Mr. Vee, I can't eat, I can't sleep, and I'm pissing off my boyfriend big-time because I don't want to have sex with him and don't give a shit about going to college next year; I just don't fucking care."

Ronnie allowed certain students, behind closed doors, to express themselves as naturally as possible, even if it meant cursing, divulging personal information, or worse; however, with the caveat that each student had to have previously earned his personal respect.

This could happen in a variety of manner and fashion...usually by good grades, athletic excellence (without being an asshole), public service, compassion (his own personal favorite quality) or generally just being a great kid. His innate and intuitive abilities never failed to recognize and frame these personal prerequisites for identification.

He would then honor his young students with the promise of complete privacy and non-disclosure; that is, unless something was either illegal (outside of smoking a little marijuana) or harmful to them, such as even slightly uttering or even inferring the dreaded "S" (suicide) word. He made that patently clear to each and everyone, and all complied.

Ronnie had then proceeded to explain to Lisa that divorce was very commonplace these days and kids were, for the most part, taking it in stride, as they, with proper guidance, had realized that it wasn't their own fault; all of their respective parents fucked up from time to time, just like the rest of the world.

Lisa, however, was so much more complicated than most, extremely emotional at times, and he knew that her current summer and senior year were going to be tough.

Ronnie loved these traits about her, though; it made for a particularly endearing young lady, and he truly was going to be there for her. He had spent the next two hours talking with Lisa about his own life, just to give her a little perspective; girlfriends he had lost, his parents who were never really happy together, and focusing on some of his various personal failures, as his accomplishments as a kid and then later in college and even later as a young adult were generally known and somewhat revered.

He realized that this coming year much time would be spent with Lisa, and other seniors, helping them to prepare for leaving home for the very first time, either via college, military service, travel/work opportunities, etc. He strongly advocated getting higher education, however, in whatever capacity was possible. The world was changing rapidly, and blue-collar work, particularly in America, was being overtaken by thousands and thousands of "non-entitled" minorities, especially Hispanics, who were more than willing to work harder and for less money than their spoiled American counterparts, and thusly succeeding in the landscaping, commercial cleaning and construction vocations.

Ronnie, as well, tried to persuade his own minority students to seek out college degrees for these very same reasons. He truly wanted his kids to have a more than decent shot at life; life that was going to be at times very cruel to many of them.

Because of the inheritance from his maternal grandfather, which wasn't a large fortune but rather a modest one, Ronin Maximus Van Valkenburg could still afford traveling to almost anywhere, and in this case easily pay for two stunning and high-class German prostitutes and a pretty decent hotel. He could also readily manage to expense his very extensive and multi-faceted private martial arts training; something he had been quite passionate about for many years, and in which he excelled but pretty much kept "under the radar".

His guidance counselor salary was modest, especially since he had been in the public school system less than a decade, but his college salary hadn't really been much better. When he left the university system to counsel high school kids, the most compelling reason was that one of his exceptional psychology students had come to the conclusion one day to just end it all, by shooting himself in the head with a .32 caliber pistol. It was the spring of this kid's sophomore year; flowers blooming, cut grass smelling like everything was brand new, Mother Nature re-introducing to everyone her passions that coincided with this season and temperatures reminding all that summer freedom was just around the corner. Even though his freshman year was stellar, and the fact that he was a highly intelligent and seemingly happy student, making great grades and hanging with friends, nothing seemed to allay the internal pressures building within this young man who had all of life yet to live.

Professor Van Valkenburg couldn't help but feel at the time that if this unfortunate soul would've come to him a year earlier, maybe even a few months, that things might've turned out in a different fashion.

Suicide is obviously more clearly read in hindsight, but alas always too late. Ronnie had taken everything he had learned from this one experience and then pored over case studies to educate himself more realistically, and had talked with several who were personally experienced with these tragedies, whether parents, siblings and even doctors. That was the singular toughest part of his research; getting to know the intimate and total heartbreak of those that felt that they could've changed the outcome. Parents, especially, were the most distraught, in that the self-guilt and failure of responsibility were overwhelming; often they even blamed each other, which had ruined many families.

Very likely, with his several years of high school counseling experience to date, Ronnie had saved one or two or three juniors and seniors from a similarly fateful outcome later in life, as several of his former kids had later emphatically confided in him that he had mattered a great deal. This was his catharsis, each time, amidst all of his encountered problems of youth and young adults.

Life was too brief a time span, when all was said and done. God had given most of us a decent shot at cherishing this gift and holding it sacred, and he fully and passionately embraced this philosophically, and thusly conceptually. He knew where he stood with his vocation, and it was so much more than being a guidance counselor by the standard designation.

A voice brought him back from daydreaming and into sharp and immediate focus, "Amerikanischer Tourist, richtig?"

He knew this young man was asking if he was an American tourist, but his intuition immediately put him on alert, as while this guy was moving towards him he was turning his head right to left, as if looking for other people, or possibly the Polizei, and his partner had simultaneously moved around the fountain in the opposite direction.

Ronnie got up quickly and replied as politely as possible, "hallo, wie geht es dir?"

The German youth then offered his left hand while reaching into the back pocket of his jeans with his right.

Back in America Ronnie had trained this scenario numerous times with his Filipino Martial Arts instructor. This was a very common move by street criminals that favored the blade; the opposite hand shake looks normal at first, but by the time one processes the greeting, the right hand is holding a knife against your throat or worse. His Kali teacher had stressed a philosophy to him at every single training session, and for both offensive and defensive purposes, "all blade, all the time!"

Ronnie took the German's left hand while glimpsing a flash of steel, and in the blink of an eye had crushed the instep of his attacker's left foot, then ducking under and through his arm, he not only snapped the radius and ulna of his attacker's left arm but also severely damaged his wrist and shoulder. The young man cried out in extreme pain, grabbing his now useless arm and dropping his knife in the process, while staggering to his knees.

His friend had just that moment come into view and looked at them with surprise and shock. Ronnie coldly looked him in the eyes, screaming "sie ficker", and then front kicked the fallen German youth so that he rolled onto his back, while his buddy fled the scene.

By now a few had started to gather, but Ronnie did not look directly at any one. Rather calmly, he picked up the knife, which was a very nice and not inexpensive Benchmade folder, slipped it into his back pocket and then walked several blocks in the opposite direction of his hotel, disposing of the weapon in an alley's trash receptacle.

He really wanted to keep this knife, mainly as a tangible reminder of his skill and extreme luck, and the fact that he had again experienced his guardian angel...adding it to the box he had planned on mailing back home the day of his departure. This package would contain the two knives he had purchased immediately upon arrival in Frankfurt, which was his habitual custom when he traveled anywhere outside of the United States; however, his logic told him otherwise and his intuition followed suit.

Later, returning to his room, Ronnie quickly canceled his remaining week's stay, claiming personal reasons having to do with his family, and arranged for a flight home that evening. He did not even want to fuck with the West German Polizei, no matter his innocence, as he knew all too well that they were extremely efficient, vicious and very unforgiving.

Upon undressing to shower, and finding his cotton shirt

sticking to his back, Ronnie looked in the mirror while peeling it off and discovered a fairly substantial, yet mostly superficial, horizontal slash across his back, which by then had largely stopped bleeding. He hoped that his attacker's knife had been clean, but would take no chances, getting the proper and complete medical care by "Doc K", his longtime friend and personal physician back home.

In the meantime, however, he called his two girlfriends from the night before and, as planned, had them come to his hotel, meeting them in the lobby and then quickly heading to the elevator.

Closing the door to his room, he immediately showed them his back and had them call a local doctor they knew and trusted to come and temporarily patch him up.

Ronnie expected to pay dearly for this emergency and, most likely, very inconvenient service, which turned out to be an extremely thorough, yet remarkably gentle procedure with no questions asked.

He was further taken by complete surprise while reaching for his money, as the doc smiled warmly, and, while holding his hand, replied "Danke, Nein, diese Mädchen sind Familie."

He gathered that these Fraulein and he were friends, which they verified after he left, and that this most certainly was not the first time for this sort of favor.

Both of the young women helped him pack and made him promise to stay in touch and to come back someday; yet collectively not really believing this would happen.

He offered to pay them, just as the night before, but again was refused. The girls genuinely liked him, and Ronnie them.

Sometimes life gives you, even if temporarily, friends that truly matter. He only hoped that both would someday find the love and happiness that they deserved. His fleeting thoughts of having them visit him back home did later make him smile, however.

The trip back to America was very pleasant, "warm" and surreal, as a marvelously chilled martini, served by a stunning flight attendant, became the perfect catalyst to the first of four painkillers the doc had slipped into his pocket, and which Ronnie would drop every two hours.

Tomorrow he would get his personal friend and physician to write a script for him after stitching him up. Even though this was an immediate concern, and warranted, Ronnie was in an almost constant state of some kind of minor injury or pain, due to his excessive training habits. He did have a predilection for the occasional "painkiller cocktail", and would not deny this; however, so far had honestly managed to maintain his great health, both physically and mentally, knowing that these "friends" were indeed highly addictive to most.

"Shit," he thought, "I was so looking forward to spending the rest of the week with those girls; fucking assholes could've killed me!"

He promised himself once again, to continue to stay sharp and focused with all future training.

II

After his medical procedures the very next day, Ronnie headed home to recuperate and soon found himself fast asleep.

He dreamed, as he was prone to do...

The white wolf was cautious as he checked the woods on his left and right and the ridge that lay ahead for any other animal activity. He traveled alone now, having lost his mate a year ago and was soon thereafter ostracized from the pack by the others, simply because he did not want to kill the younger Alpha male who had coveted his place and hierarchy. He could have very easily, though, as this white wolf was exceptionally intelligent and courageously fierce; life, so far, had proven exactly that, time and again.

He moved ahead and felt a presence that made him stop, with hackles raised, and sniffed the air. His eyes carefully scanned his immediate environment and he saw something move ahead.

By now he had reached that ridge, with its sloping sides, birch and pine trees in abundance, and then he saw her.

She was magnificent, almost his size, with raven fur that had streaks of light coffee and copper colors; he had never in his life seen such a beautiful female but it was her hazel eyes that had completely paralyzed him. They were transfixed upon his very own deep blues with intensity never before experienced. He stood completely still.

She advanced towards him with such a confident demeanor

that he was mesmerized, still finding himself not being able to present a posture of dominance so readily accomplished in past encounters.

Something told him to just not move. She slowly approached his face with hers and then sauntered to his left, just two feet away, circling slowly, feeling his body heat and giving him hers.

He knew that there was a fatal point of no return if he let her get behind him, as she could kill him more easily being out of sight.

Still, he did not move, his heart beating a steady and powerful cadence.

The white wolf had never encountered an Alpha female of this size and demeanor and his mind was racing in several directions, all at once, with a cosmic passion that belied all he had ever known.

He stood very still as she accessed his right side. Her scent was just sublime and he started to relax ever so slightly.

She slowly touched her nose to his right shoulder, confusing him to no end, yet opening up feelings that he had never experienced at any time of his existence. Then, with the grace of something most definitely divine, she rested her chin on the back of his neck, leaving it there for a full five minutes, breathing slowly with him until both of their hearts finally found each other.

Then and there, they were mated for life. It was his singular most satisfying experience ever!

III

Lisa was Ronnie Vee's very first counseling session of the new school year, her last, as she would be graduating next spring. Her parents had finally separated during the summer, with her dad moving out, and it was crushing her spirit, more now than ever. She was such a beautiful and vibrant young lady, barely 18 years of age, but he was again seeing those revealing and disturbing signs of her inner conflicts, which had begun last spring, and now actually manifesting themselves in her outward appearance and demeanor.

Ronnie thought to himself, with a semblance of prayer, "I so hope that I can help her find some reasoning and inner peace with all that's happening", and it was not going to be easy; this he knew very clearly.

"Hi honey, pull up a chair, sit next to me," as he greeted her.

Lisa was obviously more stressed than their last spring's counseling session, and he knew that his words could mean the world to her; at least he wanted as much.

"I'm worried about you Lisa, to say the least, and would like you to just sit there and listen to me, just ten minutes or so; then, I'll want you to let me know how you're feeling...and I mean truthfully. This will be more revealing than what we had discussed the last time, and for a good reason, honey. Trust me."

She nodded in agreement, knowing full well his cryptic request, and her hopeful eyes let Ronnie know that she was more than appreciative to be there.

He began, "As you know, I was a college professor just ten years ago, and, while I thought that I'd really like it, something happened that changed my life and subsequently my professional ambition."

"I had a wonderful young student in my Psychology 101 class. His name was Remy, and my God was he something else. I could tell from the very first class, just by a couple of his questions, that this kid was extremely intelligent and creative, and that he was most likely going to go far in life. Very nice, very polite, and seemed to be very happy; and, very well suited for this discipline that I so love."

"He excelled to the point of me asking him at the end of the semester if he would possibly be interested in being my assistant the following year; that is, if he continued in his studies of psychology, which he had on several occasions led me to believe."

"Remy was surprised and yet very flattered, I could tell, and the look on his face that afternoon convinced me to believe that I was in exactly the place for which I was destined."

"I felt as good as I ever had, especially since grad school. I sensed as if I had contributed, in some small manner, to a young man's future hopes and happiness."

Lisa started to say something, and Ronnie very gently allayed this with his smile and by touching the back of her hand, ever so gently.

He continued, "Well, the school year came and went, as did summer, and before you knew it the fall semester was in full swing and Remy, once again, excelled in my class, this time Abnormal Psychology."

Ronnie paused, caught up in a momentary reverie, and Lisa left him alone, to "reappear" when he was ready. She recognized, very astutely, something was going to be said by him that was going to be bad, if not outright shocking.

His eyes were starting to glaze a bit as he furthered.

"Remy was not the same kid I had met the year before. Something was different about him, something had changed over the summer, and although he had completed all of his assignments and helped me with a few students that needed tutoring, I could tell that he was battling something inside his head."

"I tried, very surreptitiously, to get him to talk about whatever was bothering him, but he would just sort of laugh it off and say that he was fine, just 'normal' college apprehensions and such."

"I had no clue as to whether this was a family issue or possibly even a romantic one, as I believed that his academic studies were going as well as could be expected."

"Come to find out, Remy was an only child and consequently had both his parents' complete focus. In many instances this is not healthy as unalleviated pressure can manifest itself later in life. It's so much easier when your brothers and sisters are fucking up, too!"

He paused, "Please excuse my cursing honey, as I'm still a bit emotional with all of this, even to this day."

Lisa smiled at Ronnie, and he nodded in return.

"He had always made straight "A"s, excelling to the point in time when his mom and dad wouldn't even acknowledge a new report card, as this was expected; at least this is what I found out through his high school counselor. Plus, his family, while not poor, counted on Remy getting an academic scholarship, as they did not have the resources to pay for his higher education."

"On an impulse, I then checked his records at our college and found out that he had received a "C" in Philosophy 101 last semester. A "C", and I thought to myself, Jesus Christ how was that possible, and how it must have crushed him so?"

"Now, I know who his teacher was, and I'd always disliked him; very arrogant, and the type that gives many of us a bad name in university academics...one of those that feels he's holier than thou, just because he's a college professor and knows that his students look up to him, sometimes to the point of worship, which is really wrong and extremely unhealthy."

Lisa shifted in her seat causing Ronnie to remark, "Sorry, honey, this is talking longer than expected."

She replied, "That's okay Mr. Vee, please continue."

"As said, I have no idea what Remy felt after receiving his final grade, but knowing that he was on scholarship, and having to maintain an excellent G.P.A., this apparently rocked his world."

"Well, I kept trying to motivate him, to reassure Remy that life does not start and stop with one grade, one disappointment. As well, I suggested he take the class over, but he could still end up with this ass of a professor and if this teacher still carried a bias against Remy, the end results might nevertheless be the same... plus, he would have to pay for this one course, as dictated by the terms of his scholarship."

"Lisa, you probably know where this is headed, but I just have to tell you. Understand?"

"I do Mr. Vee, really I do."

"That spring, Remy's fourth semester, he told me that he needed a break from being my assistant, to give him a little more time to concentrate, and that he would continue the very next fall semester, his junior year."

"Of course, I said that was fine and thought that it was a good idea, but I should've known better."

"In hindsight, which is where we all suffer with these tragedies, as we often blame ourselves, I should've known."

Lisa knew exactly where her beloved counselor's talk was headed, and held her arms close to her chest.

Ronnie continued, "Remy did not want to interact with me, that's why he begged off from continuing as my assistant; he could not face me."

"Two weeks later the news spread through campus like wildfire; he had shot himself in his own bed, when the dorm was apparently nearly empty due to a school function. Where the hell he got that gun, I have no idea, but he did and the rest is history."

"I was absolutely shaken, just devastated beyond what I had ever experienced at that time, as the pure tragedy of this young man's life, snuffed out like a candle, was too much to bear."

Lisa's eyes had filled with tears, but she remained silent and kept her composure.

"Of course, after the initial trauma started to subside, then the aftershocks began, starting with Remy's parents coming to my school to gather his personal belongings and such."

"I met with them, and all I could say was that their son was such a great kid and that I had respected him greatly."

"Small words for their now dead boy, and they had little effect, which stands to reason."

"The rest, as they say, is now history, Lisa."

"I heard later that they ended up divorcing, which is not that uncommon. Parents will often place blame on one another, as it's an escape and coping mechanism."

"That's the real tragedy with suicide, Lisa; it's those you leave behind, all those lives shattered in your wake."

"Remy's demons were vanquished with one pull of a trigger,

yet he began an avalanche that ultimately destroyed others…not fair, honey, not fair!"

Ronin Maximus Van Valkenburg, as that was now exactly how formally he felt, let these last words sink into Lisa's very soul.

They both remained silent for a minute or two, and then Lisa very quietly spoke.

"Mr. Vee, I'm so sorry for what happened, and I feel badly for your student Remy; but do you think that I would do something like that? Is this why you told me this story?"

She continued, "I know I've felt awful for several months, but I could never do something like that. Never!"

He then gazed so hard at Lisa that he could see the apprehension in her eyes.

"Honey, this is precisely why I told you this; you may seem alright at this very moment, due to the fact that I've occupied your brain for the last half hour and given you some sort of escape from the present, but rest assured that unless you truly come to terms with your parents' impending divorce, and sooner than later, things could have a way of building up and developing into a much worse situation for you. You could very well not realize this consciously, and that, my young friend, is the real danger."

Ronnie then held both of her hands in his and looked into her eyes, with as much love as he could gather and without seeming inappropriate, as he knew all too clearly that this young lady was very vulnerable, to say the least.

He knew and respected his craft well, and greatly valued the myriad relationships with all of his kids.

He continued, "Okay, you say this and I believe you. However, suicide, Lisa, is the third leading cause of death for people between the ages of 10 and 24. Think about that. In many cases, simply talking about our crises can help immeasurably."

"Regarding your parents' situation, I want you to know that it's not anyone's fault, and no one has failed anyone else. Your dad and mom are human, and they will make mistakes, just like all of us, throughout their lives. It's God's way, and that it to forever evolve as best as we can. People drift apart, for various reasons, and the fairytale of a perfect marriage is just that."

"You will always have me to help you, to encourage you, and to love you. Rest assured, honey, this is exactly why I wanted to be in this role that I so revere and adore; here in high school, to possibly help before it's too late, like it was in poor Remy's case. Do you have any idea of how many times I wished that I had known my young student before he came to college? How many times that I felt that I could've possibly saved him?"

Lisa closed her eyes nodded her head in somber agreement.

"You are welcome here anytime, but this is what I ask of you, and that is, I want to see you every single Friday for the rest of your senior year, during your free time, of course, and even if only for five minutes. I want you to look into my eyes and tell me how you honestly feel. We can both take this week-by-week, and evaluate where we are. Okay?"

Ronnie added, "And one more thing, I have a dear older friend who had counseled me on several occasions. He's kind of like an adopted father to me, and I love and trust him completely. He has even confided in me and confessed something pretty serious, and I promised I would take his secret to my grave!"

"You see, sweetheart, none of us are perfect. None of us, save for Jesus Christ."

"If you feel the need to talk with this doctor, or another counselor friend of mine, I will go with you if you want. However, if you can convince me and yourself that life is getting better, then we shall keep all of this and what we discuss just between us."

Lisa started to smile, if ever so slightly, and Ronnie took the initiative.

"Tell your mom you love her, and tell your dad." They are hurting, in their own way and will appreciate knowing that their oldest kid is safe. You understand me, honey?"

"And, look out for your little sister and brother, they really look up to you."

Lisa got up to leave, and on this very rare occasion Ronnie allowed her to hug him tightly, for just a few seconds, and he could tell that she was feeling slightly better than when she arrived. That had made all the difference to him; these small steps towards recovery, that was key.

When Lisa left, he closed the door to his office and secured its lock. He then kissed the Saint Michael's medal that he wore 'round his neck and gently placed the gold cross, similarly revealed, between his thumb and index finger.

Facing the Rosary hanging from one of his framed angels, he then, with tears in his eyes, prayed for God's continued blessing and care of Remy's soul.

IV

Ronnie's meeting with Lisa had lasted two very emotional hours and had completely exhausted him; so much so, that he took a pain killer and poured a particularly ambitious martini into his favorite iced chalice.

His recounting to her of his college student's suicide, and a couple of other personal experiences, was extremely draining, yet sobering and empowering for this young lady who had everything to live for, but took its dedicated toll on him, her trusted confidant.

He was completely spent, letting the ever so sweet ceremony and taste of his cocktail influence the Percocet dissolving rapidly into his appreciative body; once again, he vividly dreamed...

She moved very cautiously, into the thick undergrowth of the forest, her dark and murderous eyes readily focused on the deer that had stopped completely still, due to its evolutionary survival instincts and conditioning.

The white wolf watched her, but his eyes were concentrated on the surrounding theater, as he well knew that deadly misfortune could erupt in a heartbeat. Life in the wild was indeed just that, and oh so very unpredictable.

Her dark body was coiled for the kill and she moved ahead to complete her intentions, but just maybe a little too recklessly.

The white wolf sprinted as fast as lightening, giving his full effort, just as the cougar sprung at his unaware mate, as she was at this exact moment completely obsessed on reaching the deer.

The big cat completely shocked her, knocking her viciously to the ground while trying to claw his way onto her back and sink his lethal teeth into her neck.

The Alpha male arrived just in time, adrenalin at its fullest with his intent to save his mate, as the thought of losing her was more than he could possibly bear.

He fought the cougar with every ounce of his cunning and strength. His mate had recovered quickly, and then had proceeded to assist him, her killer capacity pushed to its limits, as she, too, could also not bear the thought of losing her champion and soul mate.

The cougar realized that he was more than over-matched with these two and darted off into the safety of the forest, howling and snarling, which cut through the air like a razor.

The Alpha female was lacerated on her back and sides, but superficially so, as her quickness and reflexes had once again saved her life.

He, on the other hand, had a few pretty deep wounds on the left side of his face, and one in particular was bleeding profusely.

His mate started in on him, immediately, licking his cuts and giving her white wolf as much as she possessed.

She nudged him to the ground, with his wounded side facing up, gently pawing and nuzzling him to get his heart rate to subside. She knew well what she was doing and he, once again, surrendered to her completely, closing his eyes and accepting her love.

She spent several hours cleaning his lacerations, and pressing her nose into his neck at first, then tenderly finding every part of his magnificent body with her kisses.

The Alpha female then led them to a small cave nearby and they slept that night, facing each other so closely that when she exhaled he inhaled, and vice-versa, ever so slowly, completing a most pure and passionate cycling of life, spirit and commitment.

They again knew their union was destiny, and both gave thanks to God for the opportunity given them by Him. This was a close call, but that's why they were together; they could handle anything life threw their way.

He awakened momentarily, kissed her very lightly, thanking his mate for everything. She sighed and smiled.

V

The next morning came much too quickly, as it always did when Ronnie dreamed so intensely. As well, these fantasies of his were seemingly becoming more and more real, in the sense that his recollections were sharper and most vivid.

Why was he dreaming of wolves? Was it because he had one of his students, a very talented artist, create an original depiction of a timber wolf for the rather significant tattoo on his back? But that was just a compelling feeling that had overcome him not too long ago, with no rhyme or reason to speak of, and he just went with his inner and spiritual flow (and, I might add, five hours under the knife, so to speak).

It's not like he ever categorically studied them, or had any real contact with this most magnificent of animals. He did remember, though, that years ago one of his girlfriends, maybe even the one that he let get away, did have a minor and related passion for them...that they were the largest of the dog or Canidae family, and were extremely "family oriented" in that the Alpha male and his mate, and all other adults in the pack, would care for and defend their pups most viciously, even against other wolves.

Ronnie also recalled that some could be as large as 175 pounds, which was one scary and fucking big-ass doggie, and that they did not like to stay in one place; and, would howl to communicate with their friends and pack members.

Pretty cool, when one actually thought about it.

He gathered his thoughts and literally willed himself into

the shower and then sauntered into the kitchen for a strong cup of coffee before driving to school, ready to take on another day of his senior students' numerous complications. However, this was exactly why he had left the college teaching ranks for high school kids...he just had to make a difference, and a difference was exactly what he was accomplishing, one heart and soul at a time.

He arrived early and found the time to engage himself in a nostalgic reverie and afterwards made a mental note call both of his sisters later that evening.

Vanessa and Valerie, his older siblings by three and two years respectively, were the complete and focused adoration of young Ronnie's life, and even after he discovered falling in "love" on a not so infrequent basis. Still, he truly valued and admired their intelligence, beauty and humor, and knew that they revered their younger brother's talents and especially his capacity for honor and compassion in much the same manner.

Vanessa was an "ancient soul" and very hard-core in that she demanded perfection from herself, and consequently all others around her. Boyfriends rarely lasted more than a few months or so, as she truly needed "older and wiser", but knew that would come later, when she was ready. Many times, and to her health's sometimes detriment, the self-inflicted chastisement of her actions and results, if they were any less than expected, would worry their mother to no end. However, she seemed to always manage quite nicely and would reply "Well, I got it done, didn't I?" Who could argue with her assessment?

Valerie was one year younger than her sister and Vanessa's complete opposite; super nice, super relaxed and almost laissez-faire in her approach to life. And she too, for the most part, would succeed in whatever she undertook and would similarly reply to anyone, "Well, I got it done, didn't I?" Again, who could argue?

The only difference in their patented responses was body language: Vanessa's cold, hard and almost combative stare, and Valerie's infectious smile.

Still, these two adored each other and especially their younger brother, and all jealously guarded the health and well-being of the three of them to an almost legendary fault!

One such time was a weekend afternoon when Ronnie, at eight years of age or so, was getting the shit beat out of him by the two older brothers that lived a block up the street, and in the very front yard no less, in front of God and anyone else who decided to watch.

As luck for him (and, apparently, bad luck for them), a neighbor girl who was there went immediately hauling ass down to the Van Valkenburg house screaming for Vanessa and Valerie.

Ronnie wasn't doing too badly fending off these two bullies, even though he was getting pounded and was crying whilst fighting (a trait of his that lasted until he was a teen), but still two on one usually never works out for the singular combatant, especially at that age and with older attackers.

Well, these two sisters made a beeline to where their younger sibling was struggling and each simultaneously snatched the brothers by their hair and bit the ever-lovin' hell out of both of them, following with a whiffle-ball baseball bat beating the likes of which this neighborhood had ever witnessed.

I mean Vanessa was swatting the skin off of both their faces and upper bodies while Valerie kept kicking each in the shins, all to the point at which both boys commenced high-tailing it into their house, crying like little girls. Thank God, their parents were not home that day, for their dad, and most likely mom too, would've administered a much greater beating. As it was, the humiliation of this event was quite enough to last quite a while.

The girls then gathered their younger brother; placing him between them, arm in arm in arm, and escorted Ronnie home where they administered to his numerous contusions, swollen lip and bloody nose. Then, running a hot bath, they most tenderly bathed and then softly dried him off and put him to bed. He slept for 14 hours, with the girls explaining all to their mom and dad.

Little known to Ronnie at that time was yet another reaffirmation of his love, admiration and respect for the fairer sex, and later in life, he would perform more than his share of noble intent and purpose on behalf of them.

Everyone in the Van Valkenburg house was more than proud, especially their parents, further uniting this family in a manner heretofore unknown.

Maybe, the singular greatest thing any parent can experience is the love and affection and caring their children have for each other, and how this behavior continues to develop and evolve throughout all respective lives.

Ronin Maximus Van Valkenburg would be reminded of this by both his mom and dad many times, and he would, in turn, promise each of them on these occasions to continue in said tradition, as it honestly was the very core of his mind, body and soul.

VI

Ronnie, once again, needed a respite from reality. He had just come out of a faculty meeting where a few of the more liberal teachers were asking that a special smoking section be created for the seniors. Hell, many of these students were still minors, which meant that it was unlawful regarding possession and purchase in this state, and carried fines and community service penalties.

What were they going to do, ask for IDs to see who was 18 or younger? And, what message were they sending to these boys and girls?

All of the harmful effects were discussed in their health classes, ad nauseam, and were widely known to all. Ever see anyone die from lung or other related cancer or emphysema...not pretty; and, these fucking bleeding heart liberal teachers were perpetuating yet another myth of "rights not being recognized". One could only surmise what their next agenda might be.

Jesus, kids were so entitled these days, and Ronnie truly believed many would suffer later in life; being pampered and cajoled in nearly everything they undertook was sending them a misleading message at the very least, and quite possibly a fatal one at the worst.

Nobody was sweating and bleeding and actually earning shit anymore, and the parents and teachers were mostly to blame.

He had two free hours from appointments, if he included his lunchtime, and took the opportunity to close the blinds in his office, put on a classical music station and set the alarm clock in his phone to wake him in 90 minutes. Removing his jacket and tie, he stretched out on his couch and closed his eyes...

The white wolf and his raven mate arrived at the river with welcome relief in their eyes, as the nearly unbearable heat was putting them both in a rare and unfriendly disposition. To make matters worse, he, trying to be surreptitious, got caught looking at the two females there already bathing, maybe a hundred yards away, and she snarled at him like he'd not heard before.

He was confused, in that he absolutely loved his mate, but knew she was somehow angry with this, and was trying to figure out what the hell just happened. He then looked at her with his pleading blue eyes and dropped his head in respect. She turned away, just for a moment, but then came back to him with love in her eyes, and licked his face, telling him that she was over it.

The white wolf had experienced quite a lot so far in his very eventful life, but had never encountered an alpha female that was this dynamic (and just maybe this crazy). He wondered if she was going to be like this all the time, but after thinking about it, felt that his mate was worth every ounce of his energy and pain, if necessary.

Once-in-a-lifetime opportunities, especially with regards to a best friend and divine love, happen...well, once in a lifetime!

This minor drama passed quickly, as the two other girls could literally feel the presence of this splendid alpha female, even as far away as they were, and decided to immediately rejoin their own pack nearby.

Having noticed their departure, his raven mate's mood changed again, very perceptively, into something he'd not experienced, but knew that the look in her eyes spelled pleasure and not pain.

The bond these two shared went deeper than anything he

could imagine. He knew he had saved her life with that cougar's attack, and, as well, recognized that she remembered this. From the very first time he had met her, he realized that there were powers well beyond their own control factoring in. He was starting to realize that God's own hand was involved, but for what purpose, remained to be seen.

Also, this particular female's background was hers and hers alone. She had not divulged anything to him thus far, and he had no clue as to her past; including previous mates and cubs, or where she was from. She just showed up in his life that one day and he was eternally grateful for her.

The white wolf was average in size, but not as big as many, weighing approximately 150 pounds and 28" tall at his shoulders, but he was long, almost 5' from his muzzle to the tip of his tail, and it was his length and speed that had helped save him in numerous battles over time.

His greatest asset, however, was intelligence; he just knew when and how to fight, as his intuition and improvisation was different and obviously better that all his previous enemies. And, as previously mentioned, this white alpha, had he sincerely desired, would still be the leader of his previous pack, but he would've had to kill the next in line and something told him it was time to move on...he was so glad of that decision and consequently allowing another of God's young creatures to live his life.

His raven mate was just a little smaller, and her hazel eyes gave an immediate impression of cunning and resolve, but also manifested a sense of cosmic spirit and love, and this was his newfound passion...she was unique from all others, and he cherished the fact that they were committed and everlasting mates.

After swimming for an hour or so, they found a large flat rock a little further downstream that had been thoroughly heated by the afternoon sun. They shook themselves from the remaining wetness and sprawled out side by side, and the warmth was just sublime.

They both fell asleep for a little while and then he was gently awakened by a most wonderful sensation...her muzzle next to his neck, gently nibbling and exhaling her warm breath across the side of his face. He seemed to recollect her doing this when they had first met, but that felt so long ago and this was incredibly new and enticing. His arousal, as well, stimulated his mate's to the point of enthusiastically nuzzling each other, taking turns for what seemed like an eternity, and covering nearly every place on each of their magnificent bodies. They both had "found" each other in a very new fashion and manner, and were united in their lovemaking to the point of their energy and flow being almost ethereal.

The white wolf was pretty sure that they were well on their way in creating new life, and, even though he had his own misgivings regarding another family, just wanted to make sure she was satisfied and content; he loved her that much.

His raven mate had the same intentions for him, although she knew that a litter of pups was not in the stars for them as she had barely escaped with her life, several years previous, in a vicious fight with a rival pack's male, who had nearly torn her insides out and had killed her mate.

It had taken her months to recover and she had known then that any future cubs were out of the question; this was one of the real reasons that she had decided at that time to follow her own path and destiny, venturing into the world all by herself.

Yes, wolves were extremely family oriented and she had loved her first mate and her pups most enthusiastically but events had *changed her young life to the point of hard decisions. This was very exceptional behavior, she knew, but it was what she had instinctively felt. Who knows, maybe she would again someday be reunited with her children, but she somehow knew that chapter had been written.*

Finding her alpha white mate had been divine, no question, and she was starting to evolve into another being; in fact, she already had. He had protected her life, with no regard to his own safety, putting her well-being first and foremost, something with which she had never experienced, at least to this extreme.

She had noticed his ferocity and commitment to only saving her and knew, again, that he was the one. Plus, they had kissed and loved each other in new ways, ways that were special and focused, and just amazing. He deserved her love and she his. This was why she had no qualms about presenting her mate with pleasures heretofore uncharted.

Why not? Life was so painfully brief, so horribly brutal and who even had a clue as to whether or not they would even survive the very next day.

This particular one was a moment in time to be remembered, cherished and referenced. This was a day that they were due, another gift from the Almighty!

Ronnie, in his blissful state, heard his alarm go off, but knew he wanted to stay in his dream, at least for a little while longer. He could feel the smile on his face and the warmth in his heart, truly knew that he was evolving, as this reverie was even more real than the last.

VII

Sifu Ty DeAmbrosia was putting Ronnie through his paces and demanding more of a flow with his double-knife skills.

"Smooth, Mr. Vee, smooth; fluid, like water...let your front kick set-up your technique, then move in and out like a cat!"

Ronnie had been studying Kali, Savate and JuJutsu with Master Ty, whose mother's parents were Chinese and Filipino, and his father's, Japanese and Italian.

DeAmbrosia's illustrious and extensive martial arts background encompassed not only all of his parents' diverse cultures, but, as well, his time studying in Paris and training under one of France's elite and very popular boxe-Francais champions. Sifu also went on to become a champion French kick boxer but had to retire from the ring after his third concussion.

He further coached and cautioned Ronnie, "You will get one, maybe two chances with the blade, if your opponent is good, and then you will need to be very lucky, my young friend."

The Filipino culture of the knife was legendary, especially in martial arts circles, and Sifu De Ambrosia made it clear to his student that truly mastering this style would help him in many ways, even his empty hand skills, but most particularly the danger and respect of the blade and how to dispel the various martial arts myths with regards to protective tactics. For the most part, knife defense was shit, plainly and simply, but still one could learn how to minimize damage with a serious amount of training...confront your fear.

Ronnie, at these moments, would inevitably recall Master Ty's words, spoken to him several years ago when they first started this very grave aspect of his training regimen, "There's a two-thirds fatal outcome in a knife fight, when both are good: one, you kill him; two, he kills you; and three, you kill each other," terrible odds, indeed!

Still, he trained hard and it showed. Sifu DeAmbrosia was an extremely tough mentor, but a fair one, and recognized that Ronnie Vee was not only naturally gifted with his technical and various skill sets, but, and as importantly, he was highly intelligent and street smart, and exhibited more than enough compassion in his heart to "spiritually justify" this deadly education, and not just with the blade, but in every other facet of fighting and survival.

When he had told Sifu of the two German youths that had attacked him the previous summer, Sifu had just looked at him, studying Ronnie's face for a few moments, and said, "Well, you're alive and well...so, you are very welcome."

Ronnie got it, and smiled and bowed his head in deference to his most cherished teacher.

They continued training, now with the various single knife templates and combinations, employing Sifu Ty's "weapons quadrant theory", which was based on the fact that literally every opponent will focus on the knife (in this case), leaving your other three natural weapons (both legs/knees and free hand/elbow) to set up a strike, with sequences designed to confuse, control, and if necessary to terminate.

Ronnie was also becoming a JuJutsu phenomenon, studying the human anatomy and the multitude of joint-locks, paralyzing strikes, throws and methods of flat out ending a fight in a matter of seconds.

More importantly, he was turning out to be extremely adept at handling multiple attackers, which was nearly always the case in a street assault. Predators were cowards by nature, and, like animals, used the "safety in numbers" concept of attack.

All in all, Ronin Maximus Van Valkenburg was evolving into a fantastic martial artist and fighter, but knew that any kind of attack could become disastrous in a second, and that too many people were extremely dangerous. And, that anyone could kill anyone, anytime and anyplace.

He had no illusions of being a superhero or movie fantasy, but just desired his own peace of mind and confidence in the event that he had to intervene on behalf of someone that he loved, or, as life would present itself, on behalf of someone unknown that needed his help, never mind his own personal safety.

Sifu DeAmbrosia loved his pupil, mostly because of Ronnie's soul and grace for God, and promised him that he would give his younger protégé everything that he could, knowing that his student and young friend would carry on a tradition of love, caring and protection for anyone deserving. Further, Master Ty also realized that he needed to pass on, by time-honored requirement of spiritual tradition, this most sacred wisdom and enlightenment, and he implicitly trusted his young protégé.

Ronnie's sense of honor for his students was fierce. Sometimes, when told of their seemingly impossible problems and life-threatening emotional stress, and the apparent overwhelming pain etched upon their faces, he just wanted to kill, but knew deep down that was another person other than himself; almost as if he were an animal in the wild that could deal with things on a most basic level when endangered, just going primal and ripping out throats.

At times, he missed the team camaraderie of his younger days of playing college baseball, and these one-on-one sessions with Sifu Ty and his solo training were sometimes hard to get motivated for. Still, the upside was so huge that he most thankfully accepted this "athletic evolution" and continued to push himself to higher plateaus.

After this training session concluded, Ronnie bid his mentor farewell, with the appropriate bowing and hands ceremony, and, as always, stated how much he was looking forward to their next.

The drive home found him in reflection...

Being in his middle 30's brought on many questions regarding his life-style: not married, so no kids, and not even involved with a woman on a very serious basis, at least for the time being. He dated, but no particular girl had ever felt right, except his college girlfriend Samantha, whom he thought was the one.

However, that was not to be, as when Ronnie had accepted his university teaching position, she made it clear that the life-style of a professor's wife was not what she had envisioned for herself, as Samantha was an energetic and driven, albeit gorgeous, business major with many vocational conquests riding in her future.

Plus, being a West Coast girl, she could not fathom life on the East; she even disliked the beaches, for Christ's sake; something which Ronnie could never comprehend, as he thought the West seashores were shit, for the most part. Mostly though, their philosophical differences were simply too much to overcome. Being young, and in her case atheist, was somewhat acceptable, as youth often was given a pass for inexperience. However, Ronnie felt that Sammy would always hold these particular beliefs, and it bothered him to no end.

She would, on occasion, ask him "Where's the real proof of God, darling?"

He would always answer in kind "Just look around you!"

He somehow knew, even going against what his heart was crying out to him, that they were destined for failure as a couple, even though their inner circle exclaimed otherwise.

Their break-up was painful, as most are, but this one was different in that physically they were perfect in so many ways, as the eyes of all of their friends had concurred. Looks can be deceiving, though, and with Samantha and Ronnie were they ever.

It was almost as if they loved each other too hard, but could never become the best of friends, and this dichotomy would eventually prevail.

His current girlfriend Lydia, a studio arts teacher at another high school, probably wasn't the one, either. A beautiful lady, to be sure, and they enthusiastically loved each other's occasional company, but again something was missing. The more time that Ronnie Vee spent with her, the more he was convinced that the fairytale romance, which he secretly desired, was not in the stars for him. His faith was strong enough, however, to assure him that God's plan would reveal itself, for better or worse, and he was truly okay with that.

Vanessa and Valerie would not press their younger sibling on his ways either, as they, above all others, understood his heart and his soul...something for which Ronnie was eternally grateful.

VIII

Even though the desire for novels and poetry had been his panacea for many years, and his real method of escape from the day to day madness, Ronnie now studied suicide with a passion that nearly matched his other academic pursuits for enlightenment, which included his continuing interest in philosophy and of course psychology with its myriad of modern concepts. The loss of his young student, way back in his college teaching days, still hung heavy in his heart and he sometimes found himself wistfully imagining what Remy would be doing today had he not taken his own life.

Thank God the last ten years or so of counseling high school seniors had obviously made an impact, as in no fatalities of this nature, but he was fully aware that several had been close; close enough with total anguish and despair that they had confided in him, before and after graduation, of their intimate thoughts, which at times had scared the life out of him.

He prayed for their souls often, and prayed for his own, as well. Sometimes he would, as many, question his faith, but only briefly. He had always known that if God did not truly exist, then "what the fuck?" It was as simple as that.

He was up to date on each of the current and over-all statistics, which were quite alarming, but it was with teens that he was centrally focused. Suicide was the third largest cause of death for kids aged 15-24, behind accidents and homicide. Even more appalling was the fact that it was the fourth leading cause of death among 10-14 year olds!

Reasons ranged from divorce of parents and violence in the home, to failure in school studies and feelings of inadequacy, to substance abuse, and rejection from friends and school mates to even the deaths of others that were well known to the victims. It also was readily apparent that today's social media explosion was a major culprit in the bullying and assassination of character, and the cowards that hid behind their respective keyboards deserved serious repercussion; Ronnie just wanted the beat the devil (literally) out of most. Hell, even the police were undermanned in this arena, with most forces allotting whomever they could to task force this epidemic of molestation and exploitation.

He also accurately knew that recognizing and reacting to teen depression and its signs was the key to saving these kids, it was that simple. However, many of these warning behaviors were similar to normal adolescent growth and development. Still, one had to pay very close attention to kids: talking about death and/or suicide, plans to hurt oneself, thinking no one really cares, previous suicide attempts (of course), alarming changes in behavior, continued despair and withdrawal from family and friends, substance abuse, extreme risk-taking, etc.

He had witnessed several of these with Lisa, which was why he was so focused with her. In hindsight, many of these symptoms were clearly there with Remy, but it was so easy to look back.

Ronnie believed, and had his own evidence, that if he would continue to present to his kids tangible coping mechanisms that felt actually possible, they would have a real chance at optimistic mental health. He also knew that the physical side of everything affected the mental, not the other way around which was common thought, and erroneous. He championed exercise and its myriad benefits for the mind, body and soul. So many did not get this and he would give the example: "one step in front of the other leads to many, and requires zero thought and very little action; however, you can talk your way out of that first step, always!"

Suicide...not one of his kids, and by the grace of God he would do everything in his power to prevent that from happening! He had been called to action...this was clearly and precisely evident.

That evening Ronnie and his girlfriend, Lydia, met for dinner at a great sushi bar, midway between their respective homes. He limited himself to a large hot sake, and Lydia did the same with her plum wine. They did find the time to go back to her house for their very passionate and much needed sexual release. Both suspected that their relationship was not the ultimate, but it sure felt right when they were together. Maybe living apart and limiting their time together was the key. At any rate, it was working for now and they did love each other, especially as friends, and could make each other laugh, something he always valued in a girlfriend.

Who knew if things would really evolve, but again, there was no timeline, at least for now.

Ronnie returned home and poured a gorgeous couple ounces of his beloved single malt scotch, letting the amber please his eyes and the aroma seduce his palate.

He sipped and thought of Lisa, Remy and the others that had come close to taking their own lives.

He prayed for his continued strength in championing their cause and felt that God was with him, especially this evening, as he easily could have fallen into a slight depression.

That was avoided, however, and again he dreamed...

The white wolf felt unsettled, somehow, and knew not the reason, as everything seemed to be beautiful in his life. His raven mate was eternal, this he knew and it was she that he adored and cherished.

A small part of his anxiety was based in her complete love of him, which was different from his previous mate, whose death had compelled him to leave his pack.

This one was different, and not just because she was a rare alpha. She had shown ferocity that he had never known from a female, and at the same time a love that went so far beyond the norm that it seemed impossible at times, but in his heart, he knew to be truth.

Still, something was really bothering him, and he felt it getting stronger and stronger.

They both moved along the ridge at a leisurely pace, every once in a while, nuzzling each other and appreciating the clear blue skies and smell of the forest.

He looked down into the valley and saw a couple of crows circling something, which he could not identify at this height. He headed in that direction with his mate following.

Now he was feeling very anxious, his heart starting to race with an impending sense of tragedy. His raven mate could sense his unease, as well, and licked his face for a few moments, as she knew he was in pain.

The crows were adding to their numbers and upon seeing what they were eating he raced hard into them, dispelling all with their shrieking echoing throughout the entire valley.

The male wolf had been dead for a while, and was most likely killed by a bear, as the claw wounds were indicative. As well, his neck had been broken by a bite, which had hopefully and mercifully ended this conflict immediately.

What was shocking though, was the female lying next to him, who had apparently died very recently. Her body was nearly *perfect except that her stomach was so withdrawn that it looked as if she had starved herself to death, lying next to her mate.*

The white wolf was crying hard and started to howl. He had never seen anything like this and was trying to comprehend the tragedy. His raven mate did all she could to comfort him, but his despair was overwhelming.

He looked at her with tears in his eyes and lowered his head. She caressed him and also howled once, but long and hard, letting all in the universe know how much she loved him.

They stayed there for a few days, grabbing sticks, branches and small rocks with their jaws, gently covering the female and her mate. It was a mystically and powerful reverence gifted to their two dead comrades. Each night they had fallen asleep breathing into each other's face, coming to yet another spiritual confirmation of their eternal union.

The crows showed no signs of returning and eventually the white wolf and his raven mate headed north.

Ronin Maximus Van Valkenburg awakened in the middle of the night, with the pillow underneath him soaked with his tears.

His recollection of this dream was perfect; so precise, in fact, that it got him to thinking of the connotations and symbolism, if indeed there were any.

He looked at his hands and discovered that they were holding a small rock and a twig.

IX

The two boys were just starting to go at it hard, trading initial punches and ripping clothes. Ronnie, upon witnessing the earlier hallway confrontation between the two, knew that it was headed towards exactly this, which was why he had resolutely followed them outside, through one of the school's back exits.

Master DeAmbrosia always said, "If you see two guys punching each other, neither one really knows how to fight." Ronnie took this into account and when he saw them grab each other again he moved in and slapped both of them, hard, right between their shoulder blades shocking each into a moment of confusion. One of the young men turned and grabbed his shirt. That was all Ronnie needed, as he then took this kid's hand, peeled it off and locked his arm and shoulder sending him directly to his knees, crying out in pain.

However, and from countless hours of JuJutsu training, Ronnie knew where to draw the line (ripping out shoulders and breaking wrists, though very possible, was definitely not needed here) and just held him there while he glared at the other kid and stared him into immediately being submissive.

The students watching all gasped in unison, and then started whispering to each other about what they had just witnessed.

"Everyone, get your asses back in there and get to class," Ronnie emphatically stated, "I will deal with them, and not a word of this to anyone, these two cannot afford to get expelled."

Both boys were particularly compliant, and kept their respective mouths shut.

Ronnie then looked at them and said, "Straighten yourselves up and meet me in my office. Justin, you go first, Richard will be right behind you. If either one of you starts this shit again, I will be a lot rougher with you, and then I will march your asses right down to Principal McBride's office."

They knew the repercussions of continuing their battle, so both were obedient.

Once all were in his office, Ronnie said "Both of you assholes take a seat, I'll be back in a minute."

He then headed out to the teacher's lounge, knowing that he would not return for at least five minutes, more likely ten. This was to make them uncomfortable with the silence and time, and reassess their actions and stupidity. Both were seniors and could possibly endanger their chances of graduation in the spring

Ronnie opened his office door very suddenly and purposely making a racket, thusly scaring the shit out of Justin and Richard, which made him secretly smile to himself.

"You fucking idiots..." letting that sink in for a few seconds, and then continued.

"You two look at each other; still hate in your eyes?"

They lowered their heads, realizing the sheer foolishness of their earlier altercation. Justin and Richard were headed to good schools after graduation and both were well aware that life was just really getting started.

He resumed, "You guys think you're tough. Fucking athletes and seniors believing they are the end-all. High school fights, and for the most part college ones, aren't shit. Everyone knows each other and no one is really trying to kill anyone. It's when they happen in the streets and bars and back alleys of bad neighborhoods where people truly get hurt, and I mean hurt badly."

He paused to let that sink in.

"Look at me. Both of you are bigger and stronger than I am, and I certainly do not look dangerous, but could've really damaged you two if I had wanted. Imagine if I had no hesitation, whatsoever, about injuring you guys. Justin, you would've suffered a fractured wrist and torn shoulder, putting you out of commission for months, and Richard, you would've fared much worse, trust me."

Ronnie continued, "Thing is, in the streets there are predators that will kill you, plainly and simply. They have a different mindset, with little or no regard for the sanctity of human life. I've run into these people before, and I am not kidding you. Just this last summer, while on vacation in Germany, two men tried to stab me right in fucking broad daylight, on a major street right in front of several other people. They couldn't care less. You hear me?"

"What happened to them, Mr Vee?" Justin inquired.

"Yeah, Mr. Vee, did you get hurt?" Richard added.

Now Ronnie knew that he had both kids "on board", and it was here that their biggest lesson was to be learned.

He began, "The years I've trained with Mr. DeAmbrosia, who's a world class expert I might add, taught me this; the better I become and the higher goals I achieve, the more I realize that I never, ever want to get in a street fight again. Richard, Justin, I am lucky to be alive and talking with you right now!"

He let that declaration sink in for a few seconds and stared at both, this time with a bit more compassion.

"As I said, those German men had no regard for myself, and I, because of the years of training I have consumed, was looking for the guy's knife before it even was visible, and that's my point; unless you know and study these kinds of scenarios, you will never even see the weapon before it's used, and then, most often, it's too late."

"Justin, I snapped the first guy's left forearm, dislocated his elbow and ripped out his shoulder, plus I had crushed his foot, and his screams and my eye contact with his partner were enough to scare him away."

"Sound familiar, you two?" It hit both of them like a ton of bricks that their earlier altercation was similar, except so much less injurious, and Ronnie could see the stark realization and relief in their eyes.

"Richard, when I stepped around the first guy to grab and eventually destroy his left arm, his right hand holding the knife slashed me across my back, which was not all that bad, but it could've been my neck instead, and that might have been a different story, especially if it was deep enough to reach my cervical vertebrae."

The office was silent, but Ronnie knew that he had made a point with them, something that he hoped would last them for quite a while. He understood, from years of study, that men between the ages of 19 and 35 were at extreme risk of getting hurt, mostly due to alcohol-induced bravado and subsequent fighting, and their abject stupidity.

He resumed, "I was treated by a physician there who was a close friend of the girls I was hanging out with, and he took good enough care of me to get me back here and then to my own specialist, who basically left the previous doctor's work alone, which was really just stitching and cleaning."

Ronnie again paused, standing up to stretch a little. Then he removed his shirt, showing the two this truth, and letting that reality sink in hard. Both were silent, and both were impressed.

After putting it back on, he continued, "But here's the thing you two; I am still pissed off by the fact that I had to leave Germany in a fucking hurry, cutting my vacation short, as I did not want to get involved in any legal issues, especially in a foreign country whose police are notoriously tough on their own people and sometimes worse with Americans."

Justin and Richard leaned forward, as they could sense that Mr. Vee had something important to add, but kept respectfully silent.

"Even though I was right in defending myself, sometimes the law is not fair, and this could be due to numerous reasons. I probably will never see those two girls or the doctor again, at least for quite a while, which is a crying shame. They were very good and interesting people, and Germany, my God, what a beautiful country."

Justin and Richard were still in rapt attention, as Ronnie concluded this life-lesson for them.

"I'm not going to say anything to Principal McBride, unless he questions me because some big-mouth friend of yours couldn't keep his or her big mouth shut. So, when you see your classmates that witnessed this shit, tell them to be quiet, for your own sake."

Richard and Justin, miraculously in unison, said "Thanks, Mr. Vee," which made all of them laugh out loud.

Ronnie scribbled something down on two pieces of paper.

"This is a note explaining why you were here; something along the lines of your first semester's classes in college, or some shit like that."

Both young men smiled.

"Now get out of here and to your classes, but first, apologize and hug each other, I mean that. You two were trying to embrace each other outside."

They got his meaning and complied.

Ronnie smiled and shook both of their hands, and not without affection, which they noticed.

They could hear him sigh as he shut the door behind them.

After school, principal McBride called him into his office. He had, of course, found out about the incident but used this time not to admonish his young counselor but to praise him.

Michael McBride was a legend in this county as a very resilient, but fair administrator. He was, as well, a large and very tough man and had the years of experience to back this up. Never, ever, had there been a single male student, including the biggest and meanest athletes, that had not feared him, which worked out pretty well in keeping order in this day and age.

He adored Ronnie, almost as a son, and looked after him often, especially when some of the school system's "rules" got in the way of rightful behavior.

He also was keenly aware of the impact this young counselor continuously was having on his high school students, as Ronnie's reputation was well regarded by many.

"You handled this well, Mr. Van Valkenburg."

McBride used his last name when making a particularly important point.

"I appreciate your concern for those two knuckleheads, and your wisdom in their continuing education," he added with a grin.

"Thanks, Michael, I appreciate that."

Ronnie only used his principal's first name when the two of them were alone; and sometimes this was when they met up in a bar, as McBride, being Irish, well one can make the conclusion as to their particular choice of social venue.

Michael was quite a boxer in his youth, and had the requisite scars, broken nose and physical demeanor to prove that. He was also cognizant of his young guidance counselor's proclivities, both with his martial arts training schedule and even his dalliances with the opposite sex. He trusted him implicitly, and took to heart Ronnie's love for his kids. McBride would "go to war" with and for him, and had done so on a few occasions, sometimes with the school board, and other times elsewhere.

Once, in a local bar, two men had the intoxicated nerve to threaten Ronnie because both of their girlfriends had smiled at him. Little did they know that Michael McBride was in the bathroom, relieving himself from one of his several Guinness Stouts, at that very moment.

Ronnie knew that he could hurt the two and didn't want it to go that far, as he also recognized these two guys felt that they could certainly kick his ass and would want to impress their girlfriends. So de-escalation, his first choice, was out of the question.

On returning, McBride saw what was happening and quietly moved behind them.

"Can I help you two little pussies?" Michael whispered in their ears, startling both.

They turned in a flash, but stopped dead in their tracks as McBride, a menacing man to be sure, had a look in is eyes that just was itching to fight. No fear, just the lust for pounding bullies and predators back into the reality of civilized society.

He continued, "I'd like to take you two outside and kick the shit out of you, but what I'd really love is to watch my young friend here hurt you in ways you've never dreamed of. Watch him send you home crying in your girlfriend's arms. That would make my day, you fucking idiots."

Needless to say, they backed away and that was that.

Ronnie adored this man and the feeling was mutual.

McBride brought him back to the present, smiling and with

fondness and gratitude, "Now, get out of here and on to your training this evening."

They bade each other farewell and Ronnie was looking forward to recounting this day's events to Sifu DeAmbrosia, as his mentor always wanted to know, in detail, how his protégé fared in the real world, no matter the incident.

This would be a good lesson in the JuJutsu philosophy of controlling opponents without too much damage.

"Fucking dumb-ass young men," Ronnie spoke to himself, as he eased into his black Porsche.

The sunshine was intense, especially through his windshield and the ride home was sublime.

Zeppelin III was in the queue, and it was more than appropriate.

Training that evening was even better!

X

The rain was pounding his roof and rattling the windows, the wind howling like a pack of wolves on this cool and stormy November Friday night, creating a surreal harmony that was thoroughly hypnotic, putting him into a dream-state unlike any he'd ever experienced. He intuitively felt that something was changing from within, and, instead of contemplating any kind of negative outcome, let whatever it was just take its course.

His earlier training session was pretty intense and Ronnie ached from the myriad of falls he had taken and given while running through the gamut of various Judo throws and JuJutsu takedown submissions.

His girlfriend Lydia was at one of her high school's basketball games and had asked him to go with her. However, Ronnie had graciously declined, stating his body's physically exhausted condition.

He really just wanted to take a prescription painkiller, sip on a very dry gin martini and soak in a nice hot bath. He had saved several from this past summer's altercation for a rainy day (or night), and now was precisely that moment, when his very tender body could appreciate and quite possibly safely benefit from this combination to its fullest extent.

Ronnie and Lydia would see each other tomorrow, anyhow, and he welcomed the relief of an evening's relaxation and a good night's sleep, as the next morning was free and clear of any significant personal or vocational obligations.

He started by settling in and amongst the cushions on his couch, looking at the marvelous dew gathering on his martini glass, letting the pain killer begin to creep into his blood stream, taking in the weather's symphony and again reflecting on his real purpose in this life. His philosophical tendencies sometimes stretched customary behavior and boundaries, but just what was normal, anyhow? Certainly not Ronin Maximus Van Valkenburg.

Ten minutes later he eased himself into a mildly searing bath filled with Epsom salts. Ronnie could still make out the wonderful resonances of this night's tempest and smiled at the instantaneous relief, breathing slowly, creating a wondrous, meditative state.

A short while later, after drying off, he found himself sitting at the foot of his bed, staring into the mirror over his bureau. Something felt overwhelming, as if there was a magnetic pull, almost as if the glass was a door into another world, beckoning, enticing and literally urging Ronnie to slip into that passageway.

He gazed, silently and with resolution. His reflection started to change shape and Ronnie just let it flow.

The white and raven mates had sorted out the weakest member of the herd and attacked with purpose and intent. The young bison was sickly and falling behind the others as they meandered through the grassy plain, grazing and heading towards the lake that lay further ahead.

It was past the prime time of mating season, so the two wolves felt fairly confident in their assault, without too much repercussion. This time, however, their perception was erroneous, as one solitary bull was still hanging around, having moved over a rocky hill, out of eyesight of the ravenous pair, in search of the herbs that he had discovered with his acute sense of smell.

The baby calf's screams coupled with its mother's bellowing brought the bull charging into the fray, blindsiding both wolves and knocking them flying, head over heels across the hard ground. That was quite enough of a very painful message as both of them instantly felt his mighty fury, most likely due to the bull's unrequited courting of another cow in the herd.

They crept away, unscathed but still starving and tired. The white male looked at his raven mate with sorrow in his eyes as he could see the hunger in hers. He led her away from the herd to higher ground where he knew they were safe.

This was yet another close call for them, and he knew that. The cougar attack, which now seemed long ago, could've killed his beautiful alpha and himself, but, because he was acutely aware and alert at that moment, they survived.

This time, however, he blamed himself and felt ashamed at letting her down. He was so hungry that he had let his logic and intuitive abilities slip, and knew that could never happen again.

The raven wolf lay next to him, curled almost in a fetal position, and fell asleep. A little while later he was awakened by a slapping sound and could not place its origin or purpose, got up very quietly, as not to disturb his mate, and went to explore.

He could smell water but knew that it was not the lake that the bison had been approaching. Over a small bluff he could see a large stream, flowing fairly rapidly from a recent rain somewhere. Most significantly, though, he spotted the dam and his muzzle started to drip with the saliva and anticipation of an extremely hungry predator.

The white wolf moved in a large circle, as to be downwind from the family of beavers and crept silently through the brush until he was nearly upon them, waiting until the exact moment when he could strike with assured success. Spotting the male working with his tail, packing the mud and letting him continue to create a noisy cover, he then sprang with all of his speed, cunning and purpose, completely surprising the beaver. With one vicious bite and twist of his head it was all over.

Even though he was famished, the white wolf carried the prey back to his still sleeping mate and placed it beside her. Moments later its scent awakened the raven wolf and, though startled, she immediately realized that unlike other alpha males this one had waited for her to eat.

She looked at him and he lowered his head in deference. She arose and went over to her mate, nuzzling him with all of her affection and gratitude. Still she did not eat, and looked for him to begin. He did not, returning her regard, insisting with his eyes, and she began slowly. When less than half of the beaver was devoured, she went over to her mate, grabbed him by his ear with her mouth and led him to finish their meal.

Even though it was just a temporary respite from their shared hunger, they both realized that a larger and truly spiritual meaning had just taken place, another affirmation of why God had brought them together. This overwhelming sense of joy completely filled their hearts, and stomachs, and they both curled up, her back to his front, and slept peacefully.

Ronnie awakened early the next morning and went into the bathroom to shave for his date with Lydia. They were going to catch a late matinee and then dinner at their favorite Italian place, which was owned by one of his friends.

He was also looking forward to their later rendezvous in the bedroom as both seemed to be physically and mentally on exactly the same wavelength when it came to their lovemaking.

Plus, she could kiss like no other!

His still tired eyes focused on the mirror there. He was startled but not dismayed by his reflection. There were a few very thin but distinct lines of gray in his full head of dark hair. At first he closed his eyes and shook his head, but when they again opened, the tones were clear, and they were most definitely still there.

What was even more disconcerting, however, these strands were not of the usual shade; they were a little creamier, almost as if they were bleached by the summer's sun.

"What the fuck," he thought.

"What the fuck," he said out loud!

XI

Lisa had good news for him and obviously needed to share it sooner than later. Through outside counseling she had made very clear and positive changes in her demeanor and behavior, and that got Ronnie to inwardly relax when she walked into his office.

There was something about this young lady that made him imagine what she would be like in several years; after college, after a significant relationship or two, after getting her career started, and just maybe after having children and possibly surviving a disastrous divorce. He could almost see the toughness starting to develop inside of her. Of course, he did not wish this hardship on anyone, but knew well how life could just continuously kick your ass. As an aside, he also thought that she would be one of those fortunate women that got better looking with age, and no cosmetic surgery would ever even be an issue or even a thought.

If he could continue to make a difference with this one, it would all be worthwhile. He knew she was special and sincerely believed that she knew, too.

Ronnie had thought about having kids, many times, but for some reason or another just didn't feel that he had ever found the right girl, never mind wife. He always followed the concept of "when you know, you know," but so far, he had never really known.

Samantha, from college, seemed at that time like she was, but love is so naïve when you're that age. And today, even though their relationship was still in its early stages, Lydia seemed to be the one every once in a while, but not always. That just substantiated his intuitive feeling for them in taking their time and effort regarding anything possibly at the next level.

Maybe someday...

"Hi honey, please take a seat," as he welcomed Lisa into his office. "You look happy," as his smile met hers.

Her beautiful black hair was cut to her shoulders, which now accentuated Lisa's face and gave the impression of her being a little older and more mature, in a very appealing way.

"Wow!" he thought to himself.

"Hi Mr. Vee, it's nice to be here and feeling good, all at the same time. She paused for a second or so and then quickly commented, "I like your hair, when did you do the streaks, they look hot?"

He grinned at her again, shrugging his shoulders as his "no-reply-reply". It was very easy to smile, with this young and very vibrant lady.

She continued, "I got accepted into State College, whoa, how about that?"

She was very happy and this made Ronnie feel as if he had made a difference, at least so far. Little did he know what her future would bring, but for now this was good enough.

"I knew you would," he said, "Congratulations!"

"You know, Mr. Vee, that counselor you suggested for me really helped; she was so thoughtful and seemed to truly understand what I was going through."

The woman Ronnie had proposed to Lisa was a longtime friend of his that he held in high regard. She had been through enough of her own tragedies and disappointments, but had survived and figured a way to channel all of her energy into counseling women, which was her passion and vocational forte. Also, she was not one of those liberated female antagonists that hated men, something for which Ronnie was equally grateful, as his own personal feelings for those types were not very complimentary; mainly, because he felt they created more harm rather than less, due to their vitriolic and pre-existing biases.

"I thought she'd be good for you, Lisa. Now, looking at you, she was definitely the right choice."

"Mr. Vee, she was wonderful, but you have made the most difference in my life. You are the one that gave me hope and held my hand when I was so low. You told me life was worth the pain, and I always believed you. Thank you so much."

She started to cry, and embraced him quickly before he could stop her. He held her, politely and not without love.

When Lisa had gathered herself, she continued, "Shit, just look at me, I'm a fucking mess."

"You are absolutely beautiful young lady, and I am so happy for this great news."

Lisa smiled at Ronnie in a manner and fashion that was new, new in ways that touched his heart and soul. "Christ," he thought to himself, "If only she was ten years older."

Then and there they connected on a previously unknown level. He knew it, she knew it, but Ronnie let it go, as he was fully aware of the emotional consequences, never mind the legal, ethical and moral ones.

"Well, I've got to go," she stated, "Got a date with a new guy this evening, but I'm really not into it; just something to do," as her voice trailed off.

He knew that her previous boyfriend was long since gone and was encouraged by her newfound joy with life and all that was there for the taking.

"Bye, honey, come see me sooner than later, keep me up to date on everything at home, and especially if any of your classes are giving you a hard time," Ronnie responded, knowing that she was better now, better than he had ever known.

Lisa started to leave but at his door abruptly turned to him, and before he realized what was happening, grabbed Ronnie's lapels and pulled him towards her kissing him on his mouth, saying, "I've always loved you, and I always will."

After she was gone, Ronnie sat on the couch in his office, took a deep breath and exhaled for what seemed like an eternity.

XII

Principal McBride sent a student to bring Ronnie to his office, and when he asked why, the young man said, rolling his eyes with a shrug, "He just asked me to, how would I know?"

Nothing along the lines of: "I'm not sure, Mr. Vee," or "I don't know, but he seemed to be in a good mood," and, certainly no humor and creativity with possibly, "I think he wants to discipline you for being too cool."

Typical of the attitude of kids today, very impolite but not really intending to be, just the way it was. Insolence like this, spoken to his father, would've brought a slap to his face and a warning about much worse to come. Michael McBride was of the same ilk as his father, but Ronnie would not hold it against this student, who was basically a good kid, just that his attitude was most likely destined to initiate a serious beating later in life. He just hoped that it wouldn't be too consequential.

Ronnie was thinking to himself, "What if someone saw Lisa kiss him, and told McBride? Jesus, would that be fucked up, how could I ever explain that?"

As it turned out, his thoughts weren't even close.

"How're you doing today?" principal McBride offered as Ronnie entered his office, immediately putting his fears to rest, as his demeanor was obviously compassionate.

His principal paused, started to add something, glancing at his hair for a moment, but let it pass.

"I'm fine, Michael, just a bit worn out, my seniors always take it out of me. Their personal problems seem so magnified in this day and age. I just hope most of them figure out how threatening and dangerous this world has become, before it's too late and they really get hurt."

"I know," McBride replied, "It's such a different environment these days, and more confusing. When we came up, everything seemed so, so straightforward; tougher, but you knew where you stood...today, it's kids that are overprotected, kept from bloodying their noses and dirtying their hands and ripping their clothes. Jesus, we're creating a nation of pussies. Everyone is on social media, not playing ball in their backyards and streets, I sometimes think that the Internet will be our ultimate downfall. Plus, the cyber bullying...well, we both know how awful that has been."

"I agree one hundred percent, Michael. I know of several senior boys that are in for a very rude awakening. We discuss these things, but they don't get it. All I can do is keep trying to reach them, trying to help them understand, but you know how young men are."

"Yes, I do," McBride responded, "And that's really all any of us can do."

He continued, "I wanted to talk with you regarding Jimmy McLaughlin."

Jimmy was a senior that had miraculously, at least until now, beaten leukemia's evil presence, after being diagnosed four years previous, but, and very sadly, was currently showing signs of decline, especially to anyone that knew him well. His body was betraying him and his grades were slipping, and not from a lack of his effort, he was just plain worn out.

Jimmy also, and most courageously, managed to get through the entire football season as an actual member of the team without sustaining any major injury. He had previously been the squad's most creative and dedicated manager and public relations facilitator, but had come to head coach Shep Romney this summer and asked to actually play.

He wanted it more than anything in life...to truly be a high school football player. This particular coach was another of God's gifts as a compassionate teaching icon, and, against his own trepidation, had let Jimmy play, under the caveat, and without Jimmy's knowledge, that his other players would carefully and surreptitiously look out for him...and they all magnificently did so.

What worried Coach Romney more so, however, was the potential of serious damage from the hits Jimmy might take in an actual game, as the other team would have no knowledge of his illness. As fate and luck would have it, however, God was looking out for all of them and, as stated, Jimmy survived the entire football season unscathed.

Literally every single student, faculty member and administrative staff in this high school had been touched by his courage and attitude and had thusly been affected in so many positive ways. Still, young minds are quick to forget, even adults, and sometimes teachers, too.

McBride badly, and emotionally, wanted Jimmy to graduate in the spring, as did Ronnie, and they needed to come up with a solution for everyone involved, including his brothers, sisters and parents; this was important, this was real life.

He spoke to Ronnie, looking directly into his eyes, "Jimmy's slipping, but apparently not quite fast enough to show alarm and gain any kind of compassion from his idiot French teacher, who at this precise moment is flunking him from what I've heard. Jesus, the kid's only a couple of points shy of passing, for Christ's sake!"

Ronnie offered an incredulous look at his friend and principal.

McBride continued, "I want you to go to Mr. Francois (and

the irony of his surname was not lost on either of them) and try to reason with him, not only on Jimmy's behalf as his guidance counselor, but as a fellow faculty member who realizes that from time to time exceptions should be made to rules when necessary, when it's just the right thing to do."

He paused quickly, and then furthered, "I cannot do this, kid (another of McBride's affections for his young counselor and protégé), it would look like a power play, especially if the school board found out."

Ronnie was thinking to himself "fucking bureaucracy", shaking his head and Michael McBride could apparently read his thoughts.

"Imagine, Mr. Van Valkenburg, the horseshit I go through as an administrator in the public school system? Sometimes I could just wring someone's neck, with the idiocy that is thrust upon us, especially these days, especially with all of the political correctness that is running rampant throughout society."

Ronnie replied, "I can only imagine, Michael," exhaling audibly, amplifying his feelings.

He continued, "I'll go see him after school today, sir, and come in early tomorrow to see you."

"That would be fine," McBride answered, "And good luck, my friend."

With that they both shook hands, which inevitably prompted a hug between these two as the mutual love and respect was well documented, and both of these men were not afraid to show their emotions, even in public.

Ronnie went back to his office to hang out for the last half hour of the day, and then proceeded to catch Mr. Francois immediately after the last school bell, as he was known to literally run out of school immediately upon said alarm, for God knows what, but that was his nature and Ronnie was going to ambush him.

Everyone knew that Jacques Francois was an odd person, but no one really knew why. Ronnie did, though, and suspected that Michael McBride did too, and if he had to play his trump card, he would.

"Ah, Mr. Francois, I was wondering if we might have a few minutes together, it's about one of your students, Jimmy McLaughlin, and I'm here to see how our young lad is faring with his French studies. You know he's graduating this June."

Mr. Jacques Francois looked as if he had swallowed some bad Beaujolais, as Ronin Maximus Van Valkenburg was not just your average high school guidance counselor, and his reputation had obviously preceded this visit. He was also keenly aware of the relationship Mr. Vee and Michael McBride shared, as was the entire faculty.

Ronnie also knew that this French teacher feared his principal, like many, and most likely deduced that Ronnie was here on McBride's behalf.

They discussed Jimmy's situation for a good ten minutes, with Ronnie trying to appeal to this teacher's compassionate side, but he could see that this was going nowhere. Mr. Francois was one of those "by-the-book" educators, and, by God, this young and ravaged kid would have to achieve a real passing grade, never mind his life-threatening illness.

Ronnie knew that Jimmy was on the cusp of not graduating, and not just with his French grade, but his other teachers seemingly were all in accordance with letting him slide and, for whatever their reasons, they were all in on him walking across that stage this coming spring, cap and gown, and his family looking proudly on. One could only imagine the multitude of emotions carrying out in that particular moment and Ronnie was going to make sure that it actually happened.

"Well, I had hoped it wouldn't come to this, but here it is," Ronnie emphatically offered.

Mr. Francois again looked like he swallowed from the same bottle of previously described wine and just stared at him with wide-open eyes, very possibly knowing what was coming.

Ronnie was an extremely astute judge of character and tendencies, and quite a lot was enhanced by his years of martial arts training and street survival; the very best paid attention to the smallest of details and by "profiling" people, well, that sometimes saved one's ass. Just ask any police officer.

At any rate, he had no real proof that Jacques Francois was gay, nor did it matter to him in the least, but he was going to take a shot at convincing him to do the right thing.

Ronnie Vee then spoke, in a very measured and deliberate manner, looking at Mr. Francois directly into his eyes, "If you flunk Jimmy McLaughlin, I will wait until the very last possible moment and simply change his grade, and I promise you that I can do exactly that. No one will ever know except you and me, and by then it will have been too late to stop our dear young boy from graduating with his friends. I said too late because your recourse at that time will most likely be filing a complaint to the school board and, again, Jimmy will have already experienced his celebration."

Ronnie paused to let that sink in and then continued, just as Jacques Francois started to open his mouth.

"And, if you do take it upon yourself to go to the school board, or even Principal McBride, I will divulge the fact that you are gay. But, that's not the real issue, as most people these days are extremely tolerant of this, as I am; however, students are vicious, and they can be particularly cruel. So, you will have that to contend with, but here's the real kicker," and Ronnie now was truly taking a chance with what he was about to say, but his intuition convincingly led the way.

"I know where you and your mates sometimes hang out, and I happen to know that the police are well aware of the drug culture there. What if our faculty heard about that? Better yet, what if Michael McBride knew of your extracurricular activities? He's a very fair and tolerant man, but he's also Irish Catholic, and I would not want his disappointment and ensuing judgment upon me. He can get you fired, you realize," which was totally rhetorical, as Ronnie knew that was common knowledge.

Jacques Francois just sat there and stared at Ronnie Vee, with venom in his eyes.

Ronnie did not blink an eye, and returned his gaze.

Mr. Francois' body language betrayed him, though, even before he could speak and that was all Ronnie needed to see.

Ronnie then added, with maybe an olive-branch touch of compassion, but that was his nature, "Look, Mr. Francois, I have no issues with you or your sexual narrative, truly I don't, as it's none of my, or anyone else's, business; however, this kid is going to graduate, and that's that!"

Ronnie then left, and not a further word was spoken.

That evening, he blew off training, which was rare, but he was going in early to meet with Michael McBride and wanted to assure him that all had been taken care of, but without divulging his exact manner and method. He knew his principal would trust him implicitly but still wanted to frame his dialogue a bit cryptically, so as not to jeopardize his friend whatsoever. The powers that be, in the public school system, were often unreasonable and very often unfair.

Michael would let it slide, this he knew.

A lot had happened very recently, starting with Lisa's surprise kiss, and then today's events. He was literally worn out, and not from his preferred physical training regimen; this was mental fatigue, and he sometimes despised it, and even feared it, as he was less in control with nefarious matters of thought and subsequent philosophical predicament and dichotomy.

After just one super-chilled vodka martini, he coasted into a reverie previously unknown, as his eyes were wide open, staring into the darkness outside his living room window.

He envisioned, yet again, the white wolf sunning himself on the massive rock by the river, letting the cool water evaporate from his coat and knew he'd seen this before, except, that the raven wolf was not there beside him this time. She was, however, swimming towards her mate, with a deliberate and smooth manner, taking her time, almost as if she was toying with him, prolonging their inevitable and passionate conclusion.

The beautiful white alpha then started to change shape, and Ronnie could feel the sun on his very own back, listening to the hypnotic sounds of the river and its environmental seduction. He was at supreme peace for the first time in several years.

As well, the raven mate was approaching, and when she arrived next to him, Lisa began nuzzling him, caressing his arms and legs, and nearly bringing him to a climax with just her touch.

He moaned and then she kissed him on the back of his neck, and this time he returned her advance, rolling over and pulling her into his lithe but very strong arms.

They made love as if this was their last day on earth, as if this was unlocking the door to another existence, another world and very possibly a new fate. She said that she loved him, again.

They slept in each other's arms for what seemed an eternity.

Ronnie woke at midnight, with the telltale signs of his nocturnal emission dampening his groin and thighs.

"Holy fucking shit," he thought to himself.

"What was that all about?" He asked out loud.

He took an extremely hot shower and washed his clothes, and even though it was late knew he needed part two of this evening's martini offering, making this redux an especially potent one.

He could smell Lisa's scent and her sex, still lingering on his body, even after his shower; very strong, very animalistic, very satisfying.

He sat still, head back on his couch, and closed his eyes, desperately wanting to revisit his dream, but to no avail. At least, he thought, this was a dream and not real life. She was too young, he knew, and would never, ever, take advantage of someone her age.

Still, something was going on and hoped that Lisa was far removed from anything facilitating any kind of behavior of this sort.

He tried thinking of Lydia, and for a while that worked. Even thought of calling her, but did not want to cause any alarm. He also felt that his actions just might betray his own feelings of this evening's amazing madness and unfaithful behavior, even though it was just a dream...or fantasy.

He made a third martini, and lo and behold this one did its magic, putting him into a blissful, yet short-lived deep sleep.

The next morning, after taking a very quick shower (if for any reason just to shake him into some sort of a more alert state) and not even bothering to blow dry his hair, he drove to school earlier than usual, to meet with Principal McBride, to assure him things looked good for Jimmy McLaughlin and not to worry.

Michael welcomed his guidance counselor with open arms and a cup of coffee, Ronnie's second of the morning.

"We're good to go with Mr. Francois, Michael," Ronnie offered, "I am certain you will hand Jimmy his diploma, just try not to cry, you big lug," he added with a wink and a smile.

McBride could not have been any happier, grinning like he had just consumed two Irish pints of ale and was about to get into yet another wicked and lovely barroom brawl.

Ronnie got up to leave and his principal thanked him again, adding, "I like the new look with your hair, sort of hip, makes you look even younger."

Ronin Maximus Van Valkenburg had no idea of what his friend was talking about, but did make an immediate beeline to the privacy of their faculty lounge.

He looked into the mirror, and did a double take. His hair had obviously dried and was filtered with streaks of blonde and white. He had not noticed earlier, as his hair had been wet and he'd been in such a hurry.

Also, his face seemed just a bit thinner, almost elongated. He chalked this up to not having shaved and the illusion of said physical appearance.

He stared, open mouthed and unbelieving.

Yet, he somehow believed!

XIII

Jimmy McLaughlin graduated that spring, on a beautiful and very warm June Saturday evening.

Principal Michael McBride handed him his diploma with tears in his eyes as the entire audience erupted in just maybe the greatest and emotionally charged and definitely the most magnificent of all cheering ever heard and experienced in this high school.

Jimmy could barely pull his weakened body across the stage, but he resolutely managed with the added help of his classmates and his pure will.

This was life, this was humanity, and this was special.

Lisa graduated, too. She was beaming and the look in her eyes when she hugged Ronnie Vee was pure affection and happiness. He only wished that he could have returned her sentiments, exactly.

Ronnie did, however, give her a quick hug and told her that he was more than proud. He also whispered in Lisa's ear that he loved her, too. She squeezed him back, not caring if anyone picked up on this exchange. Ronnie was somehow just fine with that.

That summer he lost both of them, Lisa to State College, and Jimmy finally succumbing to his dreaded disease.

Although the funeral of one of their own kids shook Ronnie and everyone else, for that matter, to the core, the melancholy residue of Lisa's going off to college was something new to him.

He knew that she needed to live her life, hell she was still just shy of only 19, and his relationship with Lydia was going as well as could be expected, but still he missed Lisa, in fact, he missed her quite a lot.

Jimmy was buried in his football uniform, helmet and all, and the story behind that was something else.

Just two weeks before his passing, Jimmy's mother had gone to Coach Romney, asking for his uniform, specifically in which to bury her son, his last dying wish. Since all athletic property is owned by the school system, the school board denied this request.

Principal McBride was more than livid when he met with his football coach telling him of their decision, cursing Irish venom and woe upon the obtuse idiots running the system. Coach Romney was incredulous with this news but had to accept everything, that is, until McBride started to grin, ever so slowly.

"Hang on a moment, coach," he said to Romney, "I'll be right back."

Five minutes later he returned with Ronnie, who happened to be there that summer morning, preparing for the upcoming school year. Coach Romney and Mr. Vee knew each other well, as Ronnie would go over and above what was the norm in getting his football players to keeping their grades up, always making the long-standing point of "Football will be over someday, and then what the hell will you do?" This was particularly meaningful for those few very good players, those who might have thought they'd have a shot at college ball, never mind the pros.

McBride had filled Ronnie in on the developing situation on their walk back to his office.

"I suppose all of the uniforms are kept under lock and key?" Ronnie asked Shep, with a very benign smirk on his face.

"Yes, during the off-season, they are all cleaned and stacked neatly in the storage facility just behind the locker room." Romney answered. "Jimmy's was by itself, though, as I thought for sure the school board would honor his mother's request. Hell, I even put his helmet with everything, just in case."

Ronnie Vee then asked, "Coach, you drive a Jeep Wrangler, don't you?"

"Yes, I do."

"Well," Ronnie continued, "I adore my Porsche, but have always wanted a Jeep, something about sitting higher and taking it off-road, just for the hell of it. Anyhow, I'd love to take it for a spin someday, if you wouldn't mind."

"Not at all, Ronnie, in fact, here are my keys, go have some fun. The top is off, so you will really feel what it's all about. I need to do a ton of paperwork in preparation for this coming season, so if you want to take it for a spin now, be my guest. I'll be here with Michael for another hour or so," looking him squarely into his eyes, with a wink and a nod.

Coach Romney handed Ronnie his keys, and pointed out his Jeep's. He also singled out one particular key, and laid them on the table in front of Principal McBride, without uttering a single word.

Ronnie grabbed them, and left the other two men to their own devices.

Less than an hour later, after supposedly taking Coach Romney's Jeep for a ride, he returned his keys with thanks and his own wink.

Nothing was said.

McBride just smiled, fully appreciating the magnificence of his two teachers.

That evening Ronnie Vee had gone to see Jimmy. What a tragic condition this kid was in, but his courage and faith never faltered.

With his dad and mom looking on, Ronnie handed Jimmy

his very complete uniform, and a note from Coach Romney, and this poor kid's look was priceless, something Ronnie Vee would always remember.

"Jimmy, this is for you, later, when you get better. You'll need it for this year's homecoming game. Coach Romney is having all of you graduating seniors suit up and meet on the 50-yard line at halftime, to celebrate your winning season. So, you'll need to make sure everything fits."

Ronnie surreptitiously looked at Mr. and Mrs. McLaughlin and nodded. They both smiled, but with obvious pain, as they knew Jimmy's days were numbered. The magnificent love and compassion at play was also not lost with them.

Ronnie Vee could only imagine their devastating agony.

That was the very last time he saw Jimmy McLaughlin alive.

He did, however, look splendid in his uniform at his wake, and Coach Romney, Principal McBride and Ronnie Vee all wept upon seeing this most beautiful image.

Nothing was ever said, nothing was ever revealed.

These three men had taken it upon themselves, in a supremely creative and most magnificently benevolent fashion, to beat the system and to bypass the utter ridiculousness of it all, especially when it had mattered the most.

Two weeks after Jimmy's sacred celebration and unification with God, Ronnie again took off for Europe, this time with his girlfriend Lydia. They traveled to Rome, Venice, Milan, Florence and Naples. However, it was the Southern Coast of Italy that impressed him the most, spending only a couple of days there, and he vowed to himself to return there and stay for a much longer period.

The Mediterranean waters and climate were something kissed from above, the creation of a very real heaven-on-earth. He could see himself living there, maybe when all vocational avenues were said and done, but he wasn't going to wait too long to return.

A week before school started that September, a letter arrived from Lisa.

> *Dear Mr. Vee,*
>
> *I've only been here a week, but already have met someone special. He's very sweet, very cute and everything that I've always wanted, so who knows, maybe I've met the right guy. What's wild is that he went to the same high school where your girlfriend teaches. What a small world. Anyhow, we'll see how this goes, but for now I am happy. I hope you are well and I cannot wait to come back and see you this homecoming. Please write to me, if you have the time, and let me know how you're doing. I miss you a lot, and will never, ever forget all that you did for me.*
>
> *Your one and only,*
> *Lisa*

Ronnie sat on his coach trying to make sense of his emotional state of being. He rationally knew this was good for Lisa, good for him, but could not shake the ache in his heart, and the sadness in his mind. He, as well, was all too aware that Lisa had not ended her letter with "I love you", and that did bother him.

"What the fuck is going on here," he said aloud to no one in particular; or, maybe he was really appealing to someone divine for any sense of clarity.

He hoped that he would find it, sooner than later.

He had to, this was apparent.

XIV

Lydia and Ronnie had gone to an early movie and had another amazing sushi dinner, again with sake and plum wine, and later made love like only they knew how, as they wanted and truly what obviously was physically and emotionally needed.

Neither of them knew where they were headed, but both seemed to be on the same wavelength as far as their current status, which was just living life to its fullest. They were becoming better friends, too, and this gave each the inner freedom and sanctuary from doubt and mistrust.

The school year had just begun and both were extremely busy with their respective responsibilities. Lydia was just as passionate about her art students as Ronnie was with his kids, and he adored this about her.

They were really getting along, as well as ever, and maybe their recent trip to Italy had helped to drive them into a higher romantic atmosphere. Time would tell.

He was happy and Lisa was beginning to fade from his conscious thoughts, ever so slowly, but knew that she would be home in October for homecoming, probably with her new boyfriend. He would cross that bridge then, however, and now would give his girlfriend his undivided attention and loving affection. Who knows, maybe she was the right one for him... maybe.

Ronnie never returned the favor of a letter to Lisa, and thought that it was for the best. She was too young, and in love, and the more time apart would ease any sort of pain with each other and hopefully dispel any doubt as to their respective paramours.

Still, it was Lisa that he had dreamed of, not Lydia. Ronnie understood the subconscious mind, as well as could be expected, especially with his background, but this was not an exact science and he knew that.

Anyhow, life was as good as could be expected and his personal training with Sifu DeAmbrosia had kicked into an even higher gear.

Ronnie's instructor was invaluable on several levels. Especially within the martial arts discipline, the higher one's skill developed, the more philosophical training became and the more realistic/scenario based drills evolved as a result. There was truly a limit on one's physical and technical growth, and all world-class practioners eventually reached these respective plateaus; however, the mind was a different story and it was here that Sifu DeAmbrosia was now focused with his prized pupil, and it was here that Ronnie knew his education truly began.

As well, Master Ty's spiritual (and religious) concepts were well suited for his continued evolution and Ronnie fully appreciated and greatly valued his teacher's intellect and wisdom.

He got to thinking about his college teaching days and the pompous philosophy professor that had given his psychology student and protégé Remy a C for his final grade several years ago, which was mostly subjectively determined. Teachers like that should be held accountable, and he wasn't blaming this man for young Remy's suicide, but was, however, holding him responsible for being an absolute and condescending, holier than thou asshole.

Ronnie thought that Sifu Ty would be marvelous in a university teaching environment, especially within the philosophical disciplines, and often told him so. He was so much more of a reality example than the numerous and sequestered, "college-only environment" faculty members whose veracity was nothing more than a piece of paper stating so. That was exactly one of the reasons he had left said situation, that and the fact that he needed to reach kids earlier in life, to catch them before they decided to dive off the tops of various buildings and bridges or fire bullets into their anguish filled bodies and overwhelmed minds.

Sifu DeAmbrosia's reply to Ronnie was forever something along the lines of "It is here that I belong, Master Vee (his own very complimentary and given sobriquet for him). You are the one that needs to help save our children, and I will be the one to look out for you. Yes?"

Master Ty would smile after his patented reply and bow, ever so slightly, which was his highest praise, indeed!

Of course Ronnie Vee understood and never took this scenario lightly, and always felt overcome with immediate and positive emotional encouragement; this is why he was continuing with Sifu DeAmbrosia, and most likely would do so as long as his beloved professor was alive, or himself for that matter.

Sunday afternoon was often a reflective period for Ronnie Vee, especially if Lydia was occupied with her lesson plans and various methods of enticing her students to further their artistic abilities, something she felt that most of them truly possessed. Some kids recognized this, but most did not.

Ronnie knew from his own experience with so many that innate, creative abilities needed to be cultured, of course, but only if the mind was at least somewhat clear of the dilemmas facing young people in America, and elsewhere, for that matter.

She, on the other hand, felt that art could and would solve these issues. Most likely they both were correct on some level.

They never argued this, but did discuss occasionally. As said, he loved Lydia's passion for her students, and she respected his. As a result, both were extremely and noticeably important in so many young lives.

This early Sunday afternoon found him behind the wheel of his black Porsche, driving to the Blue Ridge Mountains that were maybe an hour from his home. The breath-taking views of Skyline Drive never failed to reaffirm the presence of God, and all of His stunning majesty was again clearly on display this warm, late September afternoon.

He headed south, windows rolled down, and delightedly absorbed all that was his for the taking: the cerulean sky, the myriad cloud formations, the valleys with their rolling hills, the rivers and streams, the ubiquitous woodlands and the many birds and animals inhabiting this unique wonderland.

He drove and drove, sometimes pulling over to stretch his legs and get an even closer look at everything available to anyone just taking the time to experience.

An hour or so later he found a secluded stop, over-looking another stunning array of perfectly placed tree lines and basins, maybe 3,000 feet in elevation. The sun was now accentuating this particular region with the intensity of summer and the accompanying breeze, just ever so slightly kissing these mountains, was perfectly sublime.

He found a very large and flat rock and stretched out, removing his shirt and shoes. Ronnie could see them as they crossed a ridge, maybe a half-mile away. Two grey wolves, rare in these particular mountains, but nevertheless here they were, as they did occasionally hunt and travel through this range, as well as the Appalachian Mountains on the western side of the Shenandoah Valley.

He was mesmerized, transfixed on the magnificence of this

pair. From what he could see from his vantage point, maybe a half mile away, the obvious male was pure white, and the other very dark. However, when the sun's light shone just right, an almost purple sheen emanated from her, just like a raven's.

"God, were they beautiful," he thought. Then it hit him, with the intensity of a wonderfully placed left hook to the body, "These are my wolves, the alpha pair from my dreams. Jesus, these are my wolves!"

Ronnie's hair stood on end and he felt an overwhelming mystical connection with everything in his immediate environment. It was almost as if he were a Native American that lived in these ranges years ago and his spiritual brother was this great white wolf.

Thoughts were racing through his head, spinning out of control, but in a manner and fashion that was not at all alarming, but rather comforting in a uncanny sort of way.

He felt God, more so than ever before.

He felt Christ.

He felt the Holy Spirit.

He felt alive.

Ronnie watched them for a little while longer, as they gracefully trotted into the lower valley and then disappeared. He kept his gaze transfixed just in case they would reappear, but they did not.

He was not disappointed, however. He was thankful for this rare opportunity to witness something so powerful, so wondrous as to lift his soul, high enough to kiss the face of His Almighty Creator.

Now he understood how some people longed to return to nature and cry, "fuck all" to the human rat race.

He understood he was a product of the modern environment: his flat screen TVs, his sports car, his condo, training facilities, restaurants, his clothes, vacations, computers, cell phones, etc., and his friends and loves.

Still, something was out here that was entirely unavailable to those that did not wonder or care; an animalistic sense of essence and belonging, where life and death was a daily concern.

The wolves were out here.

Ronnie fell into a very deep slumber, hypnotized by these mountains and their divine power.

The white wolf and his raven mate were intrigued by the human, apparently fast asleep, and cautiously went up the mountain to explore. Typically, they avoided these creatures like the plague, but in this case the white wolf felt a very deep and compelling urge to get a closer look, even at the risk it might entail. His raven mate was also curious but stayed several paces behind him, as she, too, was interested but much more afraid.

Humans were their mortal enemies, always had been and forever would be. As well, she was exhibiting, more and more often, her evolving habits of attentiveness; she probably would never forget almost losing her life to that cougar because of her then lapse in judgment.

The white alpha stopped twenty yards away and just watched; no sound could be heard, as the very still and hot afternoon air seemed to hang in the balance, gathering everything in a stationary moment, capturing something extraordinary, to be preserved for whatever God had planned.

Ronnie slept very soundly, almost as if he was drug-induced, which of course he was not. He had no idea, whatsoever, of the two silently observing him, which was a good thing, as they were potentially deadly.

The white wolf crept closer and closer, and his mate cried a very subtle message to him, but it did not matter. He had to touch him; he just had to.

He sniffed, ever so faintly and then pulled his head away and just stared. Then the white wolf looked at his raven mate with wonder in his eyes. Nothing needed to be said at that point. It was very much like the feeling he had when they were swimming and he could see his reflection in the water, just looking back with exactly his own face and eyes.

The wolves then quietly left, with the white one turning back once more, almost as if to see that this was not a dream.

A mile deeper into the mountains he stopped and looked at his mate, with tears in his eyes. She comforted him as only she knew, reaffirming their most incredible bond, their true love for one another, but she recognized that something had changed with him, and even in her. This human was somehow connected with her mate, however impossible that may be, and she suspected that she was similarly affected.

Ronnie heard the howls in his sleep, and sat up quickly. He felt an overwhelming sense of peace and clarity as he searched for the source of the calls. He knew their origin and just wanted one more glimpse of the pair, but that was not to be. They were gone and that was that.

Still, he was grateful for the earlier experience. He then put his shirt and shoes back on and climbed into his Porsche. It was still sunny but starting to cool rapidly, as this elevation had its own mind about the temperature.

He started back down the mountain, appreciating the other side of the highway's panorama, just as splendid as the earlier drive's opposite scenes had presented.

He thought of Lisa. Maybe it was the white wolf's raven colored mate that reminded him of her. Seeing both of them traveling as a pair compelled him to wonder what a life's dedication to another just might entail.

So far, he had not a clue, but it was a very intriguing concept and he smiled at the possibilities.

Lydia was such a gorgeous woman with everything to offer, and with whom much to gain...but something seemed to be missing, and he could not put his finger on that. He also was reasonably sure that she felt the same.

Lisa was a dichotomy to be sure, and the uncertainty of someone so young was obvious.

Ronnie glanced into his rearview mirror.

A tuft of white, wiry hair fell from his, which was now almost entirely sun-bleached blonde.

He also noticed a smudge on his cheek, as if he'd been kissed by something with a slight hint of earth on his muzzle.

XV

Homecoming had become an event that Ronnie anticipated as his returning students, no matter how long they'd been gone, usually had encouraging updates of their respective accomplishments and general happiness. On a few notable occasions, heartfelt words such as "you really saved me", or "I'm here today because of you", completely validated his reason and purpose for counseling this unpredictable age group.

He'd always known that leaving college teaching to actually become a major factor in the guidance and development of 16, 17 and 18-year-old kids was his calling. True, his former student Remy's suicide was the obvious catalyst, but as the years passed by, Ronnie came to the inevitable conclusion that he would've ended up doing this, anyhow.

These returning alumni invariably, and at different degrees of significance, were living proof of the value of someone that understood and cared...it was just that simple, and oh how marvelous the results.

Ronnie did not view himself as any kind of saint. He was much too grounded for that kind of notion and coupled with his penchant for women (although he had finally learned to "behave" in a monogamous relationship) and his predilection for the occasional "painkiller/martini cocktail" and infrequent street fight, he knew he was perfectly human, and basically normal.

He did, though, comprehend as well as anyone the teenage mind, and made it a point of evolving with this inexact science, furthering his study and recognizing changing social and cultural patterns within this framework.

His older sisters Vanessa and Valerie were also helpful in that they, too, appreciated their younger brother's passion and worth with high school kids, and made it a point to let him know how proud they were. They both clearly understood that he needed their intelligence and resulting opinions from time to time, and was not afraid to ask for their respective advice.

All in all, Ronin Maximus Van Valkenburg was making a real difference in people's lives.

Homecoming Saturday afternoon was finally here, and Lydia was going with Ronnie, with the caveat that he had to reciprocate with her own high school's same event the very next week.

She had driven to his house early that morning so they could ride together, and have some quality time in bed together.

The late October sun was doing all it could to prevent the people in attendance from freezing, as the temperature had dropped into the upper 30's, but it was a clear and beautiful panorama, nonetheless. The collective mood was noticeably positive and many former students had decided to be there.

Ronnie scanned the stands for Lisa, whom he could not find. Still, he believed she would be there and allowed the numerous students saying hello to him take over his thoughts and further his already pleasant mood.

Lydia, stunning as always, was amused by the double takes from the guys, but she was used to this environment and the behavioral patterns of young men. Ronnie was equally entertained and fully appreciated his girlfriend's wit and charm as much as her natural beauty; and, he well knew her passion.

"Why not Lydia?" he thought.

Then he heard a voice behind him, "Hello Mr. Vee."

It was Lisa, and although she looked very pretty there was something different about her countenance. Her face looked a little heavier, he thought, and she was wearing a large coat, too big for her slender figure, which seemed strange, even in this weather.

"Hello Lisa, it's great to see you," he replied.

Lisa looked at Lydia for a moment and then introduced her boyfriend Bradley to him.

He looked at Ronnie with a wary eye but extended his hand, nonetheless.

Ronnie then introduced Lydia and she acknowledged Lisa's boyfriend, who indeed was a former student and offered, "Nice to see you again, Bradley, I understand you're playing lacrosse at State?"

He replied, "Of course, why shouldn't I be, I'm on scholarship." which really rubbed Ronnie the wrong way.

There was something about this kid that was not right, and he felt that Lisa might have found herself in yet another relationship dominated by her partner. Her body language and overall demeanor suggested this, exactly. Plus, he caught Bradley looking at him several times, almost sizing him up. This young man was obviously a well-conditioned athlete, and his posture suggested quite a bit of power and attitude.

"Well, Lisa, let's get going, I'm looking forward to meeting some of your friends," Bradley stated, "Nice to see you again, Ms. Montgomery," and with that he rushed Lisa away.

She looked over her shoulder at Ronnie and shrugged her shoulders, almost as if apologizing.

Lydia quietly said to Ronnie, "I never liked that kid. He was typical of those privileged, upper-class lacrosse boys who never seemed to get into any kind of trouble, because of their stature and culture."

"I recognized the type, honey, and he's trouble...this I know!"

Ronnie continued, "Something was different about Lisa, but I cannot put my finger on it."

"Well I can, darling," Lydia replied. "She's pregnant."

Ronnie stopped dead in is tracks and turned to his girlfriend. "You're kidding me."

"No honey, I'm not, and this I know."

Ronnie could clearly see that Lydia was telling the truth and felt awful for Lisa. Jesus, she was only 19 and now this. God, she just started college, and had the world in front of her. She could only be maybe eight weeks into her pregnancy. He could not believe that a guy like Bradley would even allow her to have a baby. Not this young, not this kind of living environment that would suffocate his college life and beyond. Ronnie figured this kid would be sexually involved with many co-eds during his collegiate years. His type supported this.

"Jesus, Lydia," he whispered.

"Yes, it's so unfortunate," she responded, and then added, "I bet she hasn't even told him."

"You're right, honey. He totally seems the type to threaten her and then drag her to an abortion clinic."

"Yes," Lydia agreed, "He's exactly that type."

Both walked a little silently and then Ronnie offered to her, "Why don't we get out of here and go back to my place? I've seen enough alumni. I'll make us dinner and we can hang in, have a couple of cocktails and watch a movie. Then, fall asleep for 12 hours or so."

Lydia looked at him with the greatest appreciation and answered, "What a beautiful thought, my darling."

Ronnie fell in love with her, maybe again, maybe for the first time, at that very moment. At any rate, it did not matter.

He was, for the first time in quite a while, feeling something deeper for a woman, and was gratefully accepting this transition; not afraid whatsoever.

They drove back to his place, in a mutual, yet blissful silence, letting their respective thoughts just meander to and fro, occasionally smiling at each other, as if on mutual and spiritual clue.

Though Ronnie's hair had turned a very noticeably lighter and blondish white, Lydia had hardly acknowledged this other than to say that she thought it looked great, and this color was extremely flattering. She had chalked this change up to a sort of mid-30's thing, and never really questioned the motive.

Ronnie, on the other hand, innately felt that something was converting with his physical make-up, due to God knows what, and just let it ride.

He suspected his dreams of the wolves, and actually seeing them, had more than a little to do with this, but what the hell was he supposed to do, keep coloring his hair back to its natural and much darker shade?

Ronnie's faith in God and His plan, was the over-riding factor in his just letting it go. And what the hell, he sort of thought it made him look a little younger. Not a bad thing.

He and Lydia shared the very best evening they'd ever had. She told him that she was also in love with him, and he, without hesitation, replied in kind.

This was what he had been searching for, what he'd always dreamed of; and, speaking of dreams, his one of Lisa was an aberration, it had to be. Maybe Lydia would appear in one, but what the hell, she was here in the flesh and it really didn't fucking matter to him...not now. Ronin Maximus Van Valkenburg was in love, once again. Hallelujah!

He made up his mind to give Lydia an engagement ring that very Christmas. It would be perfect, and maybe the two of them could go to some tropical place to celebrate the holidays. Or, he had always wanted to take a vacation train trip across the southern border of Canada, and maybe that would be beyond romantic.

The next day found both of them more or less staying in bed, drinking Bloody Marys, occasionally getting up for a snack, watching movies and making love like they were in a brand new relationship.

"Wow," he thought to himself, "This woman is fabulous."

The heavy rains, later that evening, prompted him to suggest that Lydia stay another night, getting up super early so she could get home and prepared for school Monday morning.

He offered a hot bath together, with a small nightcap and a very early bedtime. Both were nearly exhausted by then, and Ronnie's suggestion was willingly accepted.

Lydia and Ronnie fell soundly asleep, having set their respective cell-phone alarms to the discouraging, but necessary, wake-up times of 5am and 6am, respectively.

He would, of course, get up with her, but in case he fell back asleep after she left, he wanted a safety net of some sort.

The look in Lydia's eyes, leaving the next morning, told him all he needed to know. They had arrived, finally, and by no real catalyst, to their apparently mutual desire for commitment.

Even though their shared circle of friends, which was rather small, always expected this, it was slightly reminiscent to Ronnie of his college girlfriend Samantha and everyone else's expectations at that time, not theirs alone, of their future together. He had never gotten used to the fact that others had it figured out, not him.

Still, he embraced this as something desired and something new, and that was more than fine with him.

He suspected Lydia felt quite the same, as she was very alike him in spirit: individual, intuitive, intelligent and a very positive outlook and gratitude for the gift of life itself. Her passions equally matched his, and Ronnie knew in his heart that this was a trait that he absolutely coveted.

That Monday, immediately after school he bought her a ring, from the jeweler that she frequented in her town. He figured it was the only way to get her size without giving his intentions away with some lame-ass, made-up excuse. He wanted to do this the right way, especially since it was her, and his, first time. He wanted the moment to be as romantic as possible, and the surprise and her acceptance to be genuine.

Not a thought of her saying no ever entered his head as some things he just knew, and believed in his instinctive acumen, completely and unequivocally.

He was only going to tell Michael McBride and Sifu DeAmbrosia. Ronnie didn't feel that his sisters could keep their traps shut, and even though he adored them to no end, knew of their proclivity to talk, especially when it was about their younger brother's happiness and accomplishments in life.

Ronnie appreciated their penchant but they would give it away, and he would then be pissed off at them.

That evening he trained with Master Ty and shared his great news, which was accepted by his mentor with tears in eyes and a most proper bow.

Same thing for Principal Michael McBride, the very next morning, and he unabashedly cried while bear-hugging his young counselor.

"Shit," Ronnie thought to himself, "Now I have to wait two months, without giving anything away."

Most likely these two men in Ronnie's life were of the mindset that he was destined for a life of bachelorhood, not that that was such a bad thing, but there would never be any children from this most compassionate and intelligent person.

Both DeAmbrosia and McBride had found the right girl the first time and each was extremely happy in their respective marriages.

Michael had no children, but that was of mutual choice going into their union.

Master Ty had several kids, and could see his young protégé also being a wonderful father.

Ronnie left his Principal's office to return to his.

On his desk, propped up against his lamp, was a letter from Lisa. He knew her handwriting.

"How the fuck did this get here?" he said out loud.

XVI

He opened the letter, very cautiously, almost as if it might be wired to explode. Ronnie somehow expected that this was not going to be good news; in fact, he just knew it.

Dear Mr. Vee,

I had planned to come and visit you today, before going back to school, but could not let you see me, not now, not how I look.

I so wanted to spend more time with you and your girlfriend at homecoming but Bradley was such an asshole. I saw him being rude to you, glancing at you with that fucked up attitude of his.

Anyhow, you may already know this, and it doesn't matter, but I am two months pregnant. Your girlfriend looked at me like she knew...she seemed very bright and was also very pretty. I am happy for you.

Later that night I told Bradley, and I had been so afraid to, he's got the worst temper. He cursed at me, like it was entirely my fault, and then said, "Well, you have to get an abortion, I can't have this hanging over my head." How awful of him, he has no concern for anyone other than himself.

Mr. Vee, I don't want an abortion, I can't, I just can't. I'm going to have this baby, and I know it means dropping out of school, but I cannot see me getting an abortion. That would kill me. Also, I really hate college; it's not for me.

Bradley slapped me, twice. My face is all puffy and I couldn't let you see me this way. I also knew you would try and talk me out of having my baby, and for all of the right reasons except the most important one...it's not my baby's fault.

I also knew that you'd go find him and kick the shit out of him, and I did not want you getting into any sort of trouble.

For some strange reason, my mom is okay with all of this. I think since dad left she needs something else in her life. Who knows what she thinks; she's my mom.

Anyhow, I will come see you soon, I promise.

I love you, always,
Lisa

"Jesus Christ," Ronnie softly said out loud to no one, except for maybe Jesus, Himself.

Ronnie was reflecting on several things: talking with Lisa, meeting with Lisa's counselor, and then beating young Bradley within an inch of his self-serving life, but knew all were of to no avail; that is, except talking with Lisa when the time was apropos.

She was right, it is a good thing that he did not see her, face swollen and all, black eyes, etc., for his emotions just might have taken over and then...who knows what?

She had matured so much in such a short period of time, and

maybe, just maybe her reasons were more sacred than one could imagine at such a young age.

Still, having a baby at 19, wow! However, many had done it before and went on to happy and successful lives, all the while bringing along a child that deserved life.

Ronnie reflected on his high school friend Melody, who had her girl at 16, and a precious and beautiful young woman she had grown into. In fact, she would be about Lisa's age now.

This was all making more sense than five minutes ago, so he decided to wait until Lisa came to see him, if in fact she would.

In the meantime, he was more than anxious to resume life with Lydia and contemplate them living together, which was a huge step for him, but he knew in his heart that this was truly what he desired.

Also, it gave him even more clarity regarding Lisa, if she needed him, as his focus was frankly elsewhere.

He went home early that day, with Principal McBride's blessing, after he had given him the quick version of Lisa's story.

Michael had looked him squarely in the eyes and had emphatically stated, "You are not to do anything to that kid; you understand me? Promise me that, my friend."

Ronnie assured him that he would not ("at least for now," he thought to himself).

McBride knew his young friend well, and wanted him to just go home and cool out.

Ronnie did just that...went home and cooled out, after texting Lydia that he was in for the night and to call him when she had the time later that evening.

He had no training, and nothing of pending importance with his high school seniors at the moment, so he made himself a fabulous pasta and salad, complimenting that with two glasses of a very hearty burgundy.

Lydia called around 8pm, as she had an after school art club meeting with her very best students.

Ronnie gave her the events of the day with Lydia responding, "I always despised that kid, and I knew he would harm someone in the future, when he was here. Hell, he left a trail of broken hearts in this high school, and I wouldn't be surprised if he had pulled this before."

She continued, "Bradley and some of the other lacrosse players were always 'holier than thou', and I just knew they were headed for real trouble. They were so entitled; one could just see it in their demeanor. I just hope they get what they deserve, at some point."

Ronnie replied very simply, "They will, babe, guys like that always run into someone tougher, someone who just doesn't care, and then they will know the real meaning of retribution."

Sometimes Lydia would get a little nervous when Ronnie spoke in this kind of cryptic fashion, but let it go, as she knew how much Lisa had needed him in the past.

He furthered, "I'm beat, honey, gonna go to bed early tonight. I wish you were here. God would I like to just curl up beside you."

"Me too, darling," she replied. "I love you, Ronnie, I really, really do."

He immediately fell in love with her all over again, and what a rush for him.

"Thanks sweetheart, and me too. Sleep well, I hope that I dream of you."

Lydia responded, "What a beautiful thing to say, Ronnie."

She too fell in love with him, immediately and even harder than ever before.

Ronnie dreamed, but not the one that he had wished for.

The white wolf had left his raven mate sleeping in the cave that they had found for the evening. He went off alone that night, as this was his favorite time for hunting, knowing that his nocturnal methods of stealth and attack were proven over the years. Plus, his mate had been extremely exhausted from the emotional perplexity of their contact with the human and needed her rest.

The moon was full and the sky crystal clear, creating an illuminated panorama, almost as if it was midday. The multitudes of stars, shining ever so brightly, added to his visual acuity.

He crept silently through the forest, sniffing for scents of predator and prey. He knew how quickly life met death here; knew from experience.

He saw them, up on the hill, and knew something ruthless was about to happen. Three red males had a female surrounded and their intentions were nothing less than devastation and killing.

Even though red wolves were smaller than greys, there were three, and that could be extremely dangerous, especially in light of the fact that this group looked as if it had been battle tested, numerous times.

They were going to rip her apart, and even though she was not his kind, something compelled him to intervene. As well, this was not indicative of his normal behavior, but he was changing, evolving, and knew that things in this world were now very different.

He crept closer and closer, staying out of sight, but well aware that their ability for smell was superlative.

The three started in on her, circling with jaws snapping, and the snarling, paralyzing. She knew this was the end; life would cease unceremoniously, horribly and all alone.

The white wolf sprang quickly, throwing one red wolf into the other, and biting whenever he could, but not concentrating on finishing any one of them, not yet, as it was pure chaos and movement was life.

The three wolves were stunned by the size and speed of their grey adversary and in a few seconds realized that leaving was the best of all options...stay and fight and die, with throats ripped out and laying in waste, bleeding out slowly and waiting for the scavengers to pick their bones clean; or, getting the fuck out of there and living another day.

They chose the latter, and most wisely, I might add, 'cause the white wolf was in such frenzy heretofore unknown to any of the animal kingdom, and especially he, that none would be left in any kind of condition of quality life.

He deliberately sauntered over to the red female.

She slowly backed away from him, understandably. However, it wasn't he that caused her uncertainty, but the raven wolf looking on maybe 20 yards away. She was the over-riding reason the red female stood absolutely still, and when the white male spotted his mate, he then knew, as well.

As quick as a flash the red wolf sprinted into the forest, as she sensed the power and attitude in the large female, and knew she'd been much too lucky thus far, not wanting to push the possibility of another deadly scenario.

The white wolf let his mate come to him, sensing that he might be in for another emotional lashing, but just the opposite was the case. She knew her partner's intentions were noble, especially in light of recent events, and was clearly showing him that she was trying to comprehend this new mystification of behavior.

She nuzzled her mate for a good several minutes, calming him down until his breathing assured her that he was okay.

He knew, and she knew. It was just that simple, and it was just that glorious.

They both trotted off to their temporary lair, to sleep and maybe dream, as these wolves now knew how.

Ronnie awakened feeling extremely rested, but with the overwhelming sense of clarity regarding last night's reverie.

He knew that it was real, and of things to come.

He also fully acknowledged that the stars might someday cross, presenting him the opportunity to avenge Lisa's trauma, but would not further think about that until it was time.

Principal McBride wanted to see him that morning, and Ronnie knew exactly why.

Michael would reiterate his warning of not going after Lisa's boyfriend, as it simply would not be worth the repercussions resulting from the advantaged status of someone that had the wherewithal to hire a battery of expensive attorneys and prosecute him into a place of which he did not deserve.

"Good morning, Michael," Ronnie greeting walking into his principal's office, with his door having already been open in expectation.

"Morning, Ronnie, how did you sleep?"

"Very well, I needed to."

"How are you feeling now, about yesterday's events?"

"Fine, Michael, I'm fine, trust me."

"I do, my friend."

Ronnie offered, and without really contemplating the reason, as he was always fairly relaxed with his older friend and mentor, "I had a dream last night, about a white wolf attacking three red wolves."

McBride sat there, staring at Ronnie for a good 15 seconds or so, before commenting.

"Of course you did, Mr Van Valkenburg, of course you did."

McBride then winked at Ronnie, adding, "Now help these seniors that need you now."

XVII

Christmas Eve found Lydia and Ronnie at Bona Roti, their favorite Italian restaurant, as serendipitous events offered the two of them nearly two weeks free from family holiday obligations, and with vacation from school lasting until several days into January.

He had booked a four-day trip to the Virgin Islands, leaving Christmas Day, and had planned to give her the engagement ring then, but could not wait. He wanted to now, and his friend that owned this fine establishment was in on the plot.

Lydia looked like a movie goddess from the 50's; hair loosely piled on top of her head, with a black scarf covering her forehead, maintaining said coif in such a provocative fashion that it took Ronnie's breath away. Her matching black dress and heels, that perfectly accentuated her legs, were stunning. Ronnie always respected and appreciated her fitness and it was never more apparent than this evening.

He was equally impressive, with black slacks and matching jacket, accented with a casual white shirt opened at the collar, and a pair of perfectly cut and fitted soft grey Beatle boots with Cuban heels; his personal favorite. And his hair, now nearly half streaked with blonde and white, almost made him appear as some rock celebrity of sorts.

As a couple, they turned many heads, and tonight was no exception. They were made for each other.

Their appetizers, Salmone Affumicato and Cozze Alla Ligure,

were delicious, with Lydia commenting, "Honey, the mussels and salmon are absolutely divine."

Ronnie agreed with a smile and a wink.

A gorgeous Chianti complimented these two dishes perfectly, and they found themselves toasting with nearly every taste.

One could literally feel the intensity and romance between the two, especially the restaurant's owner Sergio, who just kept grinning each time he checked on their progress.

Dinner would be Pollo Marsala con Fungi and Sogliola Pescatora, two of their favorites.

Sergio had them seated in the very small and private wine room, which was their intimate favorite. The candlelight was soft and incredibly intoxicating. Lydia and Ronnie, whenever possible, sat side-by-side facing slightly inward towards each other, their personal custom, and tonight was no exception.

Their waiter was perfect, appearing at just the proper times throughout their dinner, and they kissed whenever the mood offered, completely lost with being in love.

After dinner Sergio returned with a presentation, on the house, of their desert du jour, which was a raspberry soufflé.

"With compliments of Bona Roti, and my very best blessing," he added with a slight, cryptic nod to Ronnie.

Lydia caught the gesture and was now a little wary, but unsure as to what exactly was happening.

The owner lifted the cover and lo and behold, an ornate and stunning sterling silver chalice, with a beautiful ring box centered just perfectly.

"Oh my God," she gasped out loud.

Sergio retreated, vanishing upon cue.

"Oh Ronnie, is this what I think it is?"

"I'm not sure, honey. I have no idea what's going on," he replied, now being barely able to contain himself.

She opened the box and was silent for a moment, then her eyes started to betray her overwhelming joy, with just a few tears.

"It's beautiful, so very beautiful," she finally managed.

Ronnie then took her left hand, as tenderly as possible, and placed the ring on her appropriate finger, adding, "Lydia, please do me the honor of accepting my proposal for marriage. I love you, completely, passionately, and forever and ever."

Her look and smile affirmed everything.

She whispered in his ear, "Let's get out of here darling, and go to your place. We can celebrate...the best way we know."

Sergio reappeared, with his continued grin in place.

Ronnie asked him for his waiter and the check, but Sergio dismissed his request with eloquent Italian body language and saying, "My friend, it is my honor and privilege to celebrate with you; may you two be blessed with the best God has to offer."

Ronnie shook his hand and handed Sergio a $100 bill for their waiter, which he accepted with a bow.

They left with seemingly all eyes in the restaurant transfixed on this beautiful pair, grabbing their coats on the way out and exchanging good-byes with many of the staff.

Lydia kept looking at her left hand, and he kept looking at her. Arriving at Ronnie's place 20 minutes later, they made martinis and went straight to bed. Both were truly in the mood, even though the events of the evening had worn them out to some degree.

They were going to be married and the magnitude of everything hit both of them immediately after making love, as both just stretched out in each other's arms, silent but loving and caressing, thinking about how life would change.

Their flight wasn't until 11am the next morning, so there was no real concern about finding sleep at the moment; however, sleep found them in a matter of minutes, both blissfully entwined, her rear end nestled into his stomach, another favorite posture for these two.

Neither dreamed.

XVIII

The beauty of pure romance can be miraculous, in that for many it's God's direct affirmation of just why we are here. You find someone you care more for than anyone else in the universe, and, if desired and blessed enough, create children to love, nurture and develop into the future of our world.

Infatuation is fun and often the beginning of actual love. If this paradigm evolves into real friendship, then you may have found paradise, here on earth.

Those fortunate enough to have experienced all of this know that during this time the sun feels even warmer, the symphony of birds even lovelier, the ocean's waves compelling beyond the norm, the seasons are more stark in contrast and the characteristics of each so much more lucid, and laughter, laughter is even a greater gift.

Thoughts become the genesis of art and other new ventures, music not only touches your soul but also caresses it, and food is elevated to an even higher taste sensation. As well, the messages of novels and poetry become even greater in eloquence and meaning, giving the person lucky enough to be in love a newfound clarity and understanding of literacy reality and life as the respective authors may have intended.

When head-over-heels in this emotional state one wants, even more so, to live life to its fullest. Many can do this without said conceptual basis, but when in maximum bloom, somehow existence is indeed easier, more manageable, greater in meaning and more fulfilling.

For Lydia and Ronnie, their promise of eternal bond was not needed for the catalyst of all previously mentioned, but even they were influenced beyond expectations. Both looked into each other's eyes with newfound wisdom, passion and even glory.

Joy had new meaning, which was just remarkable, especially for Ronnie, as now in his mid-30's he had more or less resigned himself to bachelorhood.

Lydia, on the other hand, somehow knew that he was the right guy, even if his intuition was not quite at the same level. Her fiancé's perception was becoming almost legendary, but most women were on a different wavelength, and she truly appreciated Ronnie's acknowledgment of this fact of life.

All in all, things would work out. Living together, preferably in a new place for each of them and possibly located midway between their respective schools, would give them a new start, without the repercussions of pre-existing "voodoo" remaining in their past homes and experiences.

The Islands, and in particular St. John, were amazing. Both Lydia and Ronnie got enough of a tan to remind them of this mini-vacation for at least a month. Ronnie's hair was now almost entirely bleached out from the sun's tropical rays, and Lydia thought he looked magnificent.

They swam, sunbathed, ate and made plentiful use of the various tropical beverages available, no matter the time of day. When the mood hit, Ronnie and Lydia would drive their rented Jeep around St. John to its opposite side and infamous Salt Pond, and use the privacy there for whatever their nude behavior called, and that they could get away with, all within reasonable provincial social behavior and decorum.

The natives were particularly hospitable and the island cuisine excellent, especially at the several small family places they got to know, dining on fresh conch, plantains, various fish and the myriad indigenous vegetables and fruits, which were sublime.

It went by in a flash, and both were just getting used to this new routine before it was all over. Of course, they discussed coming back as soon as possible, and Ronnie suggested a honeymoon return, which was excitedly agreed upon by Lydia.

However, his statement begged the question from her, "Okay, my love, when do we want to get married?"

He replied, "How about next Christmas, we'll be off for the holidays, and the idea of sunbathing when everyone else is freezing is appealing, no?"

She smiled, another affirmation.

Ronnie added, "Or, we can get married in Italy this summer. Have our first honeymoon there, and our second one here."

Lydia was even more enthusiastic about this idea, and her kiss proved so.

Neither wanted a big wedding, and so then and there they planned on getting married as soon as school ended next spring, with an immediate two-week return to Italy.

They felt like teenagers again...how glorious!

Back home, life resumed as normal and New Years Eve was a very quiet affair for both, entirely spent at Ronnie's place, with cocktails, dinner, dancing (yes, another personal favorite of theirs) and champagne at midnight with the two reaffirming their vows of eternal love, affection and caring.

He had never felt happier in his life. The same for Lydia, and both agreed to start looking for a new place as soon as possible.

That night, with Lydia at his side, Ronnie dreamed again.

The white wolf also dreamed.

Even though he loved his new mate beyond anything he could remember, he still missed, at times, his former pack; the group howling, hunting, and the general day-to-day family camaraderie and care for each other.

Also, he had been adamant about breaking tradition with normal behavior and eventually not accepting and allowing his pack's Omega wolf to be mistreated. In his family, this lower class wolf was a scrawny female who could not and would not fight her way back into the normal hierarchy, as many had done with other packs, accepting her station in life. The female wolves were particularly vicious and nasty to her at first.

This white wolf was different, and for some odd reason could not tolerate her getting abused, even though he knew that it was a way for various pack members to vent their frustrations and anger, and was actually a healthy existence in all wolf families.

He had intuitively evolved with this female, letting her eat first, not last, and daring anyone in his order to challenge him.

He somehow knew that this was aberrant conduct, but also felt strongly that this was the way it was going to be; just as simple as that.

Every so often he would have to put down a challenge from another, and again, usually it was one of the females, whom he hated fighting, but did so, if called upon.

His mate was extremely tolerant of his actions, as she also somehow knew that he was right.

He missed his former mate. She was beautiful and a wonderful mother to their pups, plus she too was an extremely progressive thinker and fighter and her actions never failed to impress upon him that she was the right one.

But that was then, and when she had died his world had

shattered, devastated to the point of him not destroying any challenge presented to him from his pack, and further not accepting any of the females amorous advances to reign with him.

He simply had left, early one morning, and had relegated himself to living life alone, almost at times looking for the fatal conclusion to his existence that surely was out there in the wild, lying in wait. If he was going to die, then it would be a glorious end to an already miraculous time here on earth.

Then a year later the raven wolf appeared, and life had again changed in ways previously incomprehensible.

She had brought a new dimension to his purpose and he had fallen in love again, when thinking this was a feeling long ago crushed and removed from his world.

Somehow life had been reintroduced, even at his age, maybe in the nick of time, and he thanked God for that.

Ronnie then materialized in his own dream.

He was floating inside a large church. Obviously, a funeral was taking place and he found himself looking down at the many faces and sadness etched upon each. He could not comprehend why every countenance was a blur, though; still, he kept searching for any kind of revelation as to what this was all about.

There was no coffin, but rather a beautifully hand-painted vase resting upon an ornate golden stand, surrounded by so many bouquets of roses, lilacs and other wonderful flowers.

He wondered why these details were clear but the faces were not, no matter how close he floated.

He then looked towards the back of the church, and in the open doorway stood the white wolf, who then proceeded to howl with a sadness never experienced.

Ronnie awoke, chilled to the bone. He looked over at Lydia who, thankfully, was lost in slumber. He was amazed by her beauty and again thanked God for bringing them together.

Life was complicated and at times very difficult, but life was amazing, and he knew in his heart he had found peace.

His dream truly bothered him, and he was freezing for some odd reason, which did not help, and his heart was racing to further his anxiety. He quietly got up and crept to his kitchen, so as not to wake her.

He found his beloved scotch and poured a half tumbler, taking it out to his living room where he sat in solitude, sipping ever so slowly and letting his body warm and nerves calm back to normalcy.

He sensed her approaching and felt her arms slowly materialize around him, letting Lydia's caresses do their magic.

He had been shaken to the core, but used every sense of his self-control not to reveal anything to his beloved girl. Ronnie even let his eyes dry without revealing their anguish.

At times, he cursed the gods of dreaming, and this was no exception.

They returned to bed and her body's heat sedated him most mercifully, and most compassionately.

XIX

That April, Lisa gave birth to her baby, a most precious little boy named Roman, with a full head of very black hair and cerulean eyes that were stunningly alert, taking in his environment from the immediate beginning of his new life.

Her entire pregnancy, and subsequent delivery, was greatly cared for by her mother, who was "fabulous", according to Lisa; along with her younger sister and brother, Ronnie's checking in with her at least once or twice every single week. She even managed to come to school from time to time and visit with him, all after normal school hours, as she did not want to advertise her condition any more than necessary and frankly was not interested in seeing anyone other than her beloved mentor and friend.

Bradley was nowhere to be found during all of this. Lisa had finally told him to fuck off, after his many threats about repercussions of not getting an abortion. She was no longer afraid of him and that empowered her beyond anything previously known. As well, her "mama bear" instincts were rapidly taking hold, further reducing him and his immature coercions to inconsequence.

She supposed that Bradley's getting his way throughout his life would factor into him thinking that it would just all go away at some point. She didn't care what he thought; she hated him and then forgot him; made her feel good, and helped her focus on the living soul inside her tummy.

Ronnie made it clear to Lisa that he was available for anything, including the delivery, but she assured him that her mother was so elated in helping her, that everything was more than fine. She said her mom was smiling all the time now, singing to herself like she had used to, and that helped to mend Lisa's broken heart over the divorce of her parents; and, it clearly helped her mother's recovery, too.

Principal McBride also knew that Lisa was coming in to see Ronnie occasionally, and helped at times to "clear the way" for her to come in unnoticed. He respected her decision to have the baby and, through Ronnie, let her know that he was also there for her. His Irish-Catholic side was very proud of this young lady, as it reminded him of his ancestors and he greatly admired her resolve.

Lydia and Ronnie went to visit Lisa one evening. Roman was now one month and both felt that Lisa would be more or less settled into her new routine as a mother.

It was immediately apparent that Lisa's mom was indeed amazing with her new grandson. Also, Lisa could not have been more loving and mature with her new baby. The environment for Roman was perfect, and this made Ronnie feel so much more at ease with his young friend's current place in life.

Lydia had found the perfect necklace for Lisa: two gorgeous sapphire and diamond hearts connected to each other representing mother and son, especially Roman's eyes, and the subsequent tears from grandma and mom verified the loving significance.

Ronnie had also presented Lisa with a check (from both of them and Michael McBride, who was more than generous, but made it clear to Ronnie in remaining anonymous) to help with expenses, and the floodgates continued. He indicated this to Lisa anyway, but with the caveat to keep her former high school principal's secret to herself.

All in all the evening was splendid, with Lydia and Ronnie

taking turns holding baby Roman, while mom and grandma proudly observed.

Ronnie thought that Lisa's mom was still an extremely attractive woman and that somewhere down the line quite possibly a new romance for her would be lying in wait.

He also noticed the look in Lydia's eyes when she held little Roman; a look that only women in their mid-30s had when the wheels of their ticking time clocks were spinning, all on their very own and with innate purpose and intent.

After two very quick hours, Lydia could clearly see the fatigue in Lisa and suggested they get going. Lisa's mom seemed to have enough energy for all, and that, Ronnie figured, was God's direct purpose for this very young grandmother at this moment in time. Roman would have wonderful care and unconditional love, from many sources, especially these two, which clearly dispelled any kind of previous thoughts of any alternative solution to his entire conception and birth.

Ronnie drove Lydia back to her place.

"Wow," Lydia exhaled.

"Yeah, I know," Ronnie softly replied.

"She seems very happy Ronnie, and I mean that. The look in her eyes when she's holding her baby is so powerful. So much love, beyond anything I've experienced."

"That's what they say, honey; nothing greater. I can only imagine."

"Me too."

They both locked eyes for a moment, and yet another message of love was immediately conveyed and accepted by both.

Ronnie could see the wheels turning furiously with his fiancé.

He smiled and then added, "It's not too late for us, honey, and I mean that. We are still very young; just that your teaching career might be side tracked for a while. What if you want to stay home and raise our baby? And, I'm all for that. This would be your choice, babe. I'm in with whatever you would want."

Lydia smiled at Ronnie, and merely stated, "I love you, so much, so very much."

The remainder of their ride was in silence. She grabbed his right hand, as her custom, and just held it in her lap, occasionally massaging his fingers and returning it only when he needed; then, retrieving and continuing this small but beautiful ceremonial "dance".

Ronnie always marveled how such a simple gesture could mean so much. In fact, and as he thought about it, there were many rituals they shared, some greater than the others, but all, all were duly noted and appreciated by him...he knew well of the divine providence of this depth of love and was equally respectful and thankful to God for the opportunity of experience. Not everyone was so lucky, and he made his gratitude known in his random prayers.

That night, after reflecting on the day's events, he penned his very first poem to his future wife.

While writing, Ronnie marveled at how it had been many years since he attempted such a labor of love; high school, he assumed, so long ago.

He had never even attempted such a paean to his college girlfriend Samantha, whom at the time seemed like life's great adventure, life's end and be-all.

They were in love then, but not like this! Something had been missing and when you're that young it's really no one's fault.

Experience is what God intended, and incessantly presented.

Lydia, my dream, my light, my love
How might I express the depth of all?

You graced my life, and held so true
I was blessed by the very heart of you

Now we find, enduring future shared
Who could have known that you and I
Would realize providence, mutual fate
I pledge my truth, my love, so great

Ronnie read and re-read this several times. This was new and uncertain territory for him, and although he always knew he was a romantic at heart, poetry was a genesis.

Before hitting the return/send key on his computer, he took a full five minutes to try to talk himself out of doing so. He was feeling amateurish and immature, not to mention extremely self-conscious.

He even sauntered to his bar and poured a quick shot of single malt, if only for the ceremony of something new. Yet, he decided to let his proven instincts take over, leaving all up to the "gods of love".

He then emailed Lydia, feeling completely satisfied in doing so.

XX

Six weeks later a very serendipitous event occurred; at least one related to the mystical forces of revenge and redemption.

Ronnie had stopped by the jewelers in Lydia's hometown to say hello to the owner who had custom designed her engagement ring, and to let him know how things were going.

Mr. Abdallah was very fond of Lydia, who had been a good client for several years. He also had personally taken the time to create the stunningly expressive necklace she had suggested for Lisa and baby Roman.

Ronnie wanted to thank him, personally. He had immediately liked Mr. Abdallah upon their first meeting, and they had shared the engagement ring secret with great fun. He also wanted to convey to this most compassionate man the look of pure joy on Lisa's face upon receiving her necklace, even if Lydia had already done so.

They talked for a good half-hour. Mr. Abdallah had three daughters and was not shy about extolling their talents and happiness, not to mention a beautiful Iranian wife, who helped to manage this family business, and it seemed to Ronnie that if all families could blueprint this, then the world would have far less issues that at present.

Ronnie bade him farewell with the promise of a return visit soon and headed to the wine and beer store Lydia frequented to grab some good Chianti for later that evening. She was cooking Pasta Alla Pizzaiola, a favorite of his, and the hearty red would perfectly compliment the very thin, lean steak that was the center of this wonderful Italian specialty.

With two bottles of Chianti Classico, a favorite of his, especially since it wasn't ridiculously priced, he headed towards his Porsche.

He opened the passenger side and gently placed the bottles of wine on the floor, so they would not roll around.

He heard a voice behind him.

"Fancy seeing you here...Ronnie."

The words and tone were obviously meant to be derisive, and were instantly recognized by him.

He turned and saw Bradley with three other guys beside him, and by the looks of their size and physiques Ronnie figured they were probably his college lacrosse teammates, but definitely athletes of some sort...one could usually tell.

"Well, hello Bradley, it's been awhile," he answered.

"I guess Lisa's had her baby by now, stupid fucking bitch."

Ronnie thought about what Bradley had just said. It bothered him quite a lot, as this idiot had no compassion whatsoever for what he was an equal party to; Lisa had delivered a beautiful baby boy and this insensitive asshole could care less.

Ronnie replied, "Well Bradley, yes, in fact she is the proudest mother of a stunning baby boy named Roman, a name of honor and courage...a name clearly not connected to his absentee father, do you not think?"

Now this was the first real shot fired across the bow. Ronnie had laid it down, with premeditated purpose.

He added, "And, oh by the way, she has healed rather well from you hitting her, especially the slaps to her face. That was rather manly of you, was it not?"

Ronnie noticed the three other guys glancing at Bradley and

then each other upon hearing this news, obviously for the first time.

Still, he knew that most likely all four of them would attack him if it got to that. You know, birds of a feather, and all that.

Ronnie was wishing that he would've held on to a least one bottle of wine, but that was then and this was now.

He ever so slowly shifted himself towards the car parked next to his, which was a large SUV, positioning his back to the driver's front door to allow for protection from behind, all the while looking into Bradley's eyes and his friends.

To get things going, as Ronnie knew that de-escalation was not in the stars for now, nor did he really want it to be, he winked at Bradley and smiled.

Then, in a split second, after seeing Bradley's eyes widen with rage, Ronnie back-handed him in the nose with his right hand, creating a crack that could be heard a block away, all the while bringing his left underneath and grabbing his throat, causing Bradley's hands to reflexively grab his, which was the exact intention. Ronnie then slipped under, hyper-extending Bradley's elbow with an arm bar and spinning him into the nearest attacker, with both falling violently into the parked SUV.

His reflexes then truly saved him, as the other two were on him in a flash with punches flying. Both grabbed his arms and Ronnie instinctively dropped his weight, causing each to momentarily lose his balance. That was all he needed, as he stomped furiously on any foot he could find. They screamed horribly and Ronnie took that moment to slip behind one, grabbing his hair and pulling his head straight back and down to the ground.

The second attacker was the only one left that had not been degraded significantly, but all it took was Ronnie's look of pure killing menace to stop him dead in his tracks.

Outside of a couple of superficial blows to his body and face, Ronnie was in rather good shape. He knew that these were still young men, which was why he had kept himself from truly injuring them, even though they may have deserved such a fate. He fucking hated bullies and these four were prime examples.

Outside of a couple of injured feet, Bradley's broken nose and dislocated elbow, and the neck strain from a perfectly executed hair takedown, they were all going to survive.

Ronnie knew the law, and was well within his rights to defend himself, exactly as how everything had transpired. He had not used his fists on anyone, which usually looked good in court as it showed restraint somehow, which always amused him in that there were far more serious ways to injure someone than a mere punch to the face.

Four men on one, well it could've been much worse for them. Still, he knew he had sent a clear and resounding message, and that was the real intent. Most likely they would never forget this "lesson", or at least for a decent period of time.

Ronnie then spoke loudly, but with control and purpose, as their whimpering was starting to truly irritate him.

"Bradley, and whoever the fuck you other three assholes are, know this...I could've put all of you in the hospital for months. Hell, I could've killed the four of you, and maybe saved the world from whatever future damage and heartache you may inflict upon those weaker than you. And that will happen, mark my words, as that is the very nature of predators, who are really cowards if you think about it, and the four of you are shining examples."

He paused for a couple of seconds and then continued, "It's your very type and character that believes everyone is so much more insignificant that you idiots are. The world revolves around you and that's it."

One of the young men started to speak and Ronnie quickly shouted, "Shut the fuck up, I'm not finished, nor am I interested in anything anyone of you has to say."

He stood there and stared at all four, making eye contact individually with each and then continued, staring at their ringleader.

"Bradley, if I ever hear of you threatening Lisa, or even talking about her in any manner, I will come find and finish you; and, I will make it look like it was legally justified. This may sound like a threat, because it is! I hope you understand exactly what I'm saying."

Ronnie started to leave and then added, "If any or all of you decide to press charges, think about it...four college athletes attacking one man; and, having not only my testimony, but Lisa's, her mother's, and maybe my fiancé, putting the final nails in your collective coffins, as she remembers Bradley's high school behavior rather well."

"The greatest thing about what just happened is that all of you know I can do what I say. That makes me feel pretty good. Now get the fuck out of here, before I change my mind, and hurt you like I want to, maybe like I should."

Ronnie watched the four of them slowly and gingerly limp to Bradley's BMW, still idling and parked nearby. As they pulled away not one looked back at him.

He sincerely hoped he'd never see Bradley again. Ronnie knew that he could kill him without too much philosophical repercussion, which was a dangerous concept. He did not want to live with something like that and driving to Lydia's asked God for forgiveness, not his first time and most likely not his last.

Lydia met him at her door and she just took his breath away. Her yellow sundress, bare feet and hair tied with a matching ribbon caused Ronnie to immediately fall in love all over again, and his countenance betrayed his thoughts which Lydia immediately read, bringing about a gorgeous smile from her, that is until she looked at him closely.

She had not noticed the swelling in his face, or the several bruises on either side, and, to add further evidence to his previous altercation, his shirt was ripped.

"What happened, honey?" was all she could say.

"Let's open a bottle of this wine and I'll tell you, but I'm fine honey, really."

She trusted him implicitly, and immediately relaxed, which helped Ronnie to do just the same.

They sat on her couch, and before Ronnie started he paused, taking time to absorb the amazing aroma drifting from her kitchen.

He smiled, "God does that smell delicious. Thanks, babe."

Lydia returned affection and said, "Tell me what happened, honey. You sure you're okay?"

Ronnie spent the next fifteen minutes recounting everything: his wonderful time with Mr. Abdallah, shopping for wine and then running into Bradley and his friends.

He left nothing out, and went into precise detail to not have to talk about it in the future, or at least with Lydia. He would decide later if Lisa should know, but for now felt that it probably wasn't going to be necessary, at least any time soon.

Lydia understood his reasoning for detail perfectly, and just listened, sipping her wine and holding his hand.

They each finished their first glass and were well into their second before Ronnie had completed his adventurous day, which had happened, literally, just down the street.

"After dinner, let's take a long, hot bath, and I'll give you a massage, honey," she offered.

Ronnie's wink and smile were his affirmation, as he was now starting to feel the aches and pains of a still young man, but not as young as he thought he was, and in the most inner recesses of his mind wished for one of his beloved pain killers. He knew, full well, that this paradigm would be in place for his entire life. He nodded to himself and exhaled slowly upon realization.

They ate an early dinner and, after his insisting on cleaning all the dishes (a trait of Ronnie's that Lydia adored), enjoyed that very enticing bath. However, it only took minutes into Lydia's massage before they found themselves making love like only they knew how: slowly, passionately, and with the true affection of very best friends.

How simply wonderful their relationship was.

Both fell fast asleep, wrapped in each other's arms and breathing ever so leisurely.

Earlier, Ronnie had predicted to himself that he would dream that night, and dream he most certainly did.

The white wolf continued to howl in the doorway of the church. The same church and same dream as Ronnie last experienced.

He still could not make out any details as to why he was there, who were the blurred faces or what was exactly going on.

He floated over to the particularly large white wolf and gazed into his azure eyes. The reflection was of himself, and most clearly defined, which made the dichotomy of the other distorted faces in this church even greater.

The white wolf could see his own image in Ronnie's eyes, as well. They stared at each other for quite a while, as if almost telepathically exchanging information.

Ronnie and the alpha male then walked side by side into

the cemetery that was behind the church. Gardens and flowers prevailed, with the antique richness of times passed. A flowing waterfall and fishpond beckoned them, on their way passing statues, gravestones and other interesting markers of those now with God.

They sat together, listening to the intoxicating flow and sound of water, feeling nature threading its way into both of their very souls and minds.

The white wolf then started to walk away but turned back to Ronnie, asking with his eyes to follow him.

Ronnie intuitively felt something uneasy, but stayed the course with his new and very unusual friend.

Another ten yards or so ahead lay a beautiful weeping willow, most majestically covering her turf. A particularly ornate stone bench was in place, just wide enough for any two that needed each other in times when found here.

The white wolf moved against Ronnie's leg and stayed there, almost as if protecting him.

Ronnie noticed an engraving in the exact middle of the bench and it took his breath away...it was the letter "L".

He collapsed into the white wolf, crying out loud, holding his arms tightly around this most magnificent animal.

The white wolf straightened his shoulders and let Ronnie's sobs find their way to conclusion, eventually nuzzling him with his nose and licking away his tears.

XXI

Lydia and Ronnie married in early August and their honeymoon was a second trip to Italy, this time for 15 days. Both appreciated that when they returned home there would be nearly two weeks to decompress before the public school system began its new year, and the resumption of their respective teaching and counseling responsibilities in full swing.

Neither had planned on a wedding this soon, but Ronnie's dream had shaken him to the core and his intuition strongly conveyed to him to convince his fiancé that it wouldn't matter if they waited or not...so, why not, and now? He loved and wanted to live with her.

It was a very small affair, with just the two of them, Lydia's best friend Julie, Sifu De Ambrosia and his wife, and Michael McBride with his. As well, Ronnie's college friend, a very progressive Methodist minister, presided over the ceremony, with his childhood sweetheart and wife by his side.

Both Lydia and Ronnie had come to the very same conclusion that they would celebrate with various members of each family and close friends when the time was right. They figured that on their honeymoon, sending announcement post cards to everyone, especially from Italy, would be perfect in that no one would call and bother them and all could let this news sink in before they returned home. Everybody else could work out their own emotional responses on his or her own time, not theirs.

Ronnie knew that his sisters would be mildly upset, but not

enough that they wouldn't understand. In fact, he suspected that when Vanessa and Valerie contemplated his actions, they would see the light, too.

Lydia and Ronnie figured that their parents would be relieved in that they wouldn't have had to spend any money. They, upon returning and getting back into the flow of everything, could celebrate with whomever in due time and whenever convenient.

They had found a gorgeous four-level town house, midway between where each had previously lived, in a newly planned "Town Center" community, and on its centrally located lake, all within walking distance of restaurants, movie theaters, shops, grocery stores, and even a gym, which got Ronnie thinking of joining to get his weight-lifting shape back into focus, as it could compliment his continued training with Master Ty.

He had never expected Lydia to go for this type of urban living, but it was her idea all the way. He absolutely loved this place and was looking forward to returning and taking their leisurely time in finishing unpacking and putting the final touches on their new home before school started.

Italy was once again stunning beyond belief. This time they had spent a full week in Venice and the remaining eight days in Calabria, with its gorgeous Southern Coast. With all the amazing food they enjoyed, both had managed to stay very much in shape, swimming and making love as often as possible...just as newlyweds should.

The weather could not have been more cooperative, and both returned with tans of golden bronze. Also, Ronnie's hair was now completely blonde, and really, almost white. Lydia thought that the Italian summer sun had finally bleached everything to its limit, but he knew better.

The white wolf in his dreams was connected to him in a

most profound manner. He did not understand the analogies, symbolism and parallels directly, but knew there was something going on that tied him into his special reveries. He sensed an evolution of sorts that belied all traditional paths.

He also sensed an impending doom that he could not dispel. Something in his deepest psyche was eating away his insides, and he desperately wanted to rid himself of any thoughts of losing such a beautiful soul.

In fact, and as most parents will attest when speaking of their children, he wanted to take the hit for either of the two women he loved, whatever that would entail.

Alas, life didn't work that way and God had his own plan, something which none of us could ever alter.

Ronnie just hoped and prayed to this same Divine Entity that he was mistaken, and that his dreams meant shit.

His faith was very, very acute, but he also got pissed at our beloved Father from time to time; Ronnie knew that many things were simply unfair.

Where was the logic in this?

Age old question...age old dilemma.

XXII

September, October and November all flew by in a flash. The comfort of their new home and truly being an integral part of each other's daily lives was better than either could've imagined.

When they went their separate ways every weekday morning, traveling to different high schools, all Ronnie could do was think of seeing Lydia that evening. Even his martial arts training was starting to take a "back seat". Fortunately, Sifu DeAmbrosia understood completely and made Ronnie take a full two months off, just to get acclimated with married life. He contemplated that his beloved mentor was yet again extremely prescient in matters of love, family and the world in which they resided.

Over the Thanksgiving holidays Ronnie and Lydia managed to finally (and mercifully) end the continued celebration of their marriage, with their respective families making the collective effort to gather at their new home, all at the same time. And while stressful, with parents and sisters and an aunt gathered there, the results were just fine.

The very next morning after Thanksgiving, and while alone in their bedroom, Lydia told her husband that she was pregnant.

His reaction was very obviously the most positive feeling that he'd ever experienced, and Lydia was just beside herself with his unabashed joy.

He then dropped his head into her shoulders and cried like a baby, with her joining him.

Vanessa and Valerie had spent the night, sending their

kids home with the grandparents, just to have extra time with their baby brother and their new sister-in-law. This proved to be serendipitous, as, upon hearing the news, the four of them found themselves in the most loving and celebratory Friday after Thanksgiving ever.

He should've dreamed peacefully that night, but alas, that was not his nocturnal fate this time.

The white wolf was summoned by his raven mate, and her howling made his blood run cold. He raced to the hilltop where she had gone to explore and upon arriving, stopped dead in his tracks, unable to process what his eyes were showing him.

At her feet were the remains of a wolf cub, obviously having been dead for quite a while, yet no visible signs of a predator's attack were apparent. It was almost as if this pup's heart had just given out, maybe after having been chased by something intent on taking its life, but never getting the chance to complete the deadly effort, due to God knows what.

The white wolf had seen much death in his life, as he knew his mate had, and was confused as to her intense grief over this. However, the more he thought about it, the more convinced he was that this was a vivid reminder of his alpha love's past... something had similarly happened to her and he did all he could to calm his grief-stricken mate.

She would not leave this pup's side, so he stood watch while she then proceeded to gather brush to cover its remains, much as they both had done with the two wolves they had previously found, seemingly so long ago. He tried to help her, but her quick snarl told him to let her be. He understood. He was evolving in manner and fashion that belied normal behavior, and somehow knew this was his destiny with her...both were on a path pre-determined by their beloved universe.

They left the next morning, but not without howling in unison, for several minutes. It was the catharsis both required.

Ronnie's sisters left the next morning, leaving their younger brother and his new wife alone to enjoy their peace and solitude, as their lives were going to change in a most dramatic fashion upon arrival of their baby nine very quick months from now.

Vanessa and Valerie knew what was in store for the couple and, from experience, figured each weekend until then was going to be most sacred and appreciated.

Lydia and Ronnie spent Saturday and Sunday talking about fixing up the baby's room, and possible names for either a boy or a girl, as they did not want to know until delivery.

They carefully made love, even though both knew it was fine to do so, but still they were cautious and gentle. Something had changed in them, literally overnight, and that was just fine. Sex was different but just as special...more spiritual, and even more intense.

Ronnie knew this was God's way.

They even discussed the logistics of Lydia continuing to teach. However, with Ronnie's small but decent inheritance, they both realized that just maybe their baby could have the benefits of a full-time mother, at least until those early pre-school years commenced.

Lydia was still young, there would be plenty of time to resume her career if so desired. And, what if there were more children? They laughed aloud at this most beloved thought.

Time would tell, and time would guide and take care of the myriad of thoughts required when needed.

They were a smart couple, but more importantly, they were a respectful one, whose love for each other and shared faith was most genuine.

XXIII

Monday, late afternoon, Ronnie got a call from Lisa's mom, and to say that it was shocking would have been a vast understatement. Baby Roman had been found dead in his crib that morning and Lisa was now missing. The news hit him like an avalanche.

Amidst her anguished sobbing, she apologized for not calling earlier and ran down the entire day's scenario, as best as she possibly could. The preliminary report was Sudden Infant Death Syndrome, but that was a quick assertion, as Roman was very healthy and nothing was obviously discernable, which did little to dispel any of the many doubts Lisa and her mom now had, and the resulting confusion and heartbreak.

Ronnie knew well of this most perplexing cause of death with infants, as, during his studies of suicide, SIDS cases came up as a causal assertion several times. He knew this could affect Lisa, and went into an immediate alarm state regarding her well-being and whereabouts.

He tried calling Lydia, who was still at her school in a parent/teacher conference, but she was not answering, and he hastily wrote a note explaining what was going on and told her to call his cell as soon as possible. He had to find Lisa before it was too late.

Ronnie had an awful feeling in his guts and his adrenaline was spiking. He grabbed his keys and went tearing ass out of the house literally diving into the driver's seat of his Porsche. He had a hunch, and made a bee-line to his high school.

On the way, he tried Lydia again, but to no avail, and then

called Michael McBride to let him know that he was on his way to their school. His principal said he'd meet him there.

The high school was all locked up for the evening, with only security lights outside and inside being in effect. He let himself in and ran straight to his office. The door was ajar and his reading lamp on. He knew in his guts what he would find. Laying on the couch was Lisa, motionless, and his heart skipped a beat. He thought to himself, "Oh no!"

She was not breathing and an opened bottle of sleeping pills lay just shy of her outstretched right hand; in her left was Ronnie's Rosary, which had been hanging on his wall.

He dialed 911, quickly putting his phone on speaker, and started administering CPR to Lisa, while giving exact details to the operator. She assured him help was now on the way.

He heard sirens almost immediately and feverishly continued with Lisa. She abruptly coughed and then violently threw up. Ronnie, in his entire life, was never so glad to see someone get sick.

The paramedics came in and immediately took over, stabilizing and then taking her to the hospital in town. Ronnie promised them he'd be there immediately, to answer any questions, just as soon as he called Lisa's mom and his wife.

Jesus, how life could dramatically change in a heartbeat. A beautiful baby called to God, with his young mother nearly following, was too much to bear. He wondered just how much one person could possibly take, and in Lisa's case, this was just too fucking unfair.

Where was God's grace, this time?

Michael McBride arrived and put both of his large hands on his guidance counselor's shaking shoulders, as Ronnie sat on his couch and calmly spoke with both women, assuring Lisa's mother that she would be okay. He truly didn't know how long she'd been without oxygen, but took a positive and very spiritual guess, just the same. He hoped and prayed that he was correct with his diagnosis, and something told him he was.

Lydia was extremely concerned for Ronnie, naturally, and his instincts had told him to spare her the vivid details, at least for the present time. As well, she breathed a very audible sigh of relief when he told her that Michael McBride was there by his side.

The truth could be revealed later, if necessary, and when everyone had the time to process.

Ronnie then left for the hospital, with his beloved principal ordering him not to come to school tomorrow.

Ronnie objected, saying "life goes on, Michael."

"Yes, it does, my young friend, but life also needs to repair itself within, from time to time, and your kids will survive a day or two without their cherished counselor."

McBride furthered, "You call me tomorrow afternoon, and I will decide whether you take another day off. And no arguments, my son. Be there for Lisa and her mom...and be there for your wife."

Ronnie, once again, immediately realized the magnitude of his principal's acumen, and the depth of his compassion and intuition. Michael McBride knew that someone needed to look after Ronin Maximus Van Valkenburg, and, at the present time, it wouldn't be Ronnie, that was patently clear.

Upon leaving, his principal added, "I'm extremely proud of you, Ronnie. It's men like you that truly make a difference, and I'm not talking about just in students' lives, here and there. I'm referring to all of us and our evolution as humans. God has a plan, and sometimes it's highly questionable, but I do know this...we are supposed to improve, plainly and simply, and you, my son, are a living example."

With that, he gently ruffled Ronnie's hair with his huge hands and left.

Ronnie Vee sat in his office for a full five minutes, managing more than a few tears, before getting up to leave. He started to return the rosary to its place on his wall, but decided to keep it in his pocket and give it to the person that needed it most.

XXIV

He approached Lisa's room with a reverence that was literally palpable, finding her mother sitting by her bedside and tenderly holding her daughter's hand in both of hers.

Lisa was obviously heavily medicated, with a breathing apparatus attached, and the look on her mom's eyes ripped at his guts. She promptly stood up and buried her head into Ronnie's shoulders, crying quietly, so as not to disturb her daughter's precious moments of unconsciousness; which, at the present, would be the only peace she would know.

"Oh Ronnie, why? Why?"

He just held Lisa's mom and gently stroked her hair.

All he could say was "We'll get through this, I promise you. I'll make sure that she'll be okay."

Nothing else was said, and he continued holding her for a while, gently stopping when Lisa's physician entered the room, a beautiful woman who could not have been over 30, and Ronnie suddenly felt very old.

She spoke to them, "We are going to keep her here under observation for several days and run a few more tests on Lisa, but her preliminary reports are good."

This brought an immediate shudder of relief to Lisa's mother, who squeezed his arms, hard.

Then the doctor looked at Ronnie, "Are you the one who administered CPR?"

He nodded his head.

"Then you are to be commended, my friend, you saved her life!"

Ronnie could only gather a blank stare in response, as this news shook him to the core. His imagination started to run away with him. What if he hadn't had his instinctive reaction to go to his office, what if he had an accident on the way, what if he hadn't known CPR? On and on and on.

He knew this could be harmful for him, so he consciously dispelled any further wandering thoughts and focused on the young girl lying on a hospital bed. Years of martial arts training had, of course, given him the tools for defending himself and others, but it was the meditation, so stressed by Master DeAmbrosia, that was kicking in, and now is when he needed it most.

Lisa's doctor left them alone, and five minutes later Lydia walked into the room, carrying maybe the cutest stuffed animal Ronnie had ever seen. She gently placed it beside Lisa's pillow, so as not to get in any way and disturb her if she moved.

Even though it was a white dog, Ronnie knew better...it was the white wolf of his dreams, with whom he now had a relationship so much greater than his reveries. Ronnie was floored and closed his eyes to clear his mind, while cautiously placing his rosary around the stuffed animal's neck. His hands trembled as he did so and Lydia held him from behind while Lisa's mom kissed him on his cheek.

The three were silent for a few minutes.

Ronnie spoke first, looking at Lisa's mom, "She's going to need pretty intensive therapy, which will most likely last for months."

He paused, and then added, "I will be glad to start with her, but am going to notify the doctor she had before. They were perfect together, and that is not as common as one might think. Maybe, between the two of us, we can help her to recover as best as possible."

Lisa's mom nodded in agreement.

Lydia then added, while softly holding Lisa's mom's hands, "I will be glad to do whatever I can. You just let Ronnie or me know. I mean this, nothing is more important."

No one spoke about funeral details...that was simply too painful. Instead, they collectively stood next to this tragic young girl and silently prayed for the most love and peace that God could deliver. Now is when it was needed most, but later is when it would be required.

Ronnie thought about how he could possibly approach this with Lisa and it brought tears to his eyes, which he most surreptitiously concealed from both women standing beside him.

Lydia, in her infinite wisdom, had brought Ronnie's favorite stationary with her, and presented it to him all the while winking and nodding at Lisa's mom, signaling for both of them to give him some time alone in her hospital room.

He wrote reverently, his thoughts coming into focus...

My Dear Lisa,

Words cannot express the intense sorrow and pain that Lydia and I share with you, your mom, baby brother and sister. We all are heartbroken, and right now all I can do is ask God to watch over Roman until you two again meet. God needs to care for you, too. None of my faith means shit unless He helps us get through this, and shows us how to possibly make any kind of sense with all that's happened.

I do know this, honey; it's best friends and loving family that will be your recovery. You may not realize it next week, or even next month, but you will next year.

> *I promise you everything I can possibly do for you, I will.*
>
> *Know that you are one of my very true friends.*
>
> *All my love and prayer,*
> *Ronnie Vee*

Ronnie was so tired when they got home, that Lydia literally helped him to undress.

He crashed in a major way, knowing that he did not have to get up in the morning for school.

He would call Michael McBride tomorrow and visit Lisa, possibly during the day, when Lydia was at school, as he needed an entire and uninterrupted evening with his new wife and expectant mother of his very first child.

Ronnie welcomed the thought of just that as sleep overtook him with the veiled fury of forces much greater than he.

He dreamed in the most vivid manner to date.

The white alpha male nuzzled his raven mate into the stunning, natural grotto that lay at the feet of the Blue Ridge Mountains. It was early December and extremely cold at night, and this was a perfect sanctuary for however long they needed. Even though their winter coats were as thick as ever, this cave added a natural shelter from the elements.

Since finding the remains of the wolf pup several weeks ago, she had remained depressed and the white wolf was sure that it had indeed been a stark reminder of his mate's past.

Day by day he would encourage her to either hunt, play around or even make love, but she would decline, at least politely, his advances. Now, he was going to do something new about all of this, something that was uncharacteristic of his species.

The white male's first act was to remind her again that she was the one. Even though he had done so now on countless occasions, it was again necessary and he did not mind. She was special, and needed him.

As she lay in the warmest corner of the cave, he put his head next to hers, close enough for her to feel his breath, and started with a very soft and low, guttural growl, that lasted only a few seconds. He then licked her face, as a continuance of his vocal sounds, showing her that the two acts were connected.

He let a few minutes pass and started again, this time on the other side of her face, and his growl was decidedly different in method. He gave her very short, and even lower, sounds than before, for a much longer period of time, quite possibly making the point of a small but necessary change in this attempt at her psychological recovery.

After administering a third approach, he continued all for a good half hour, and finally sensed that she was relaxing like he'd not seen in quite a while.

Then, he put his powerful jaws around her throat, ever so gently, showing her to trust him, and that all would be fine. He stayed there for just a minute, then released her to lay her head back down.

Lastly, the white alpha nuzzled and kissed her everywhere on her body, and in places she'd never experienced. She trusted him and let her senses run wild.

Never had any male spent this kind of time and effort with her, and when he was done, she signaled to him that it was his turn.

She was finally back to her normal self, and they both slept a most peaceful night.

Ronnie awoke the next morning. His dream told him that his personal therapy with Lisa would most likely be the path she'd covet.

Not anything more than "doctor/patient" decorum, but she trusted and loved him, and it would be necessary for her.

He was anticipating becoming a father, and was more in love with Lydia than he could've ever imagined. This would keep him grounded and focused on Lisa's eventual recovery, along with Michael McBride's, Lydia's and Lisa's mom's unified help.

Life. How tragic, at times?

XXV

Baby Roman was buried on a Sunday, a full two weeks later, to allow for Lisa's release from the hospital, as her mom knew that she just had to be involved in this most sacred ceremony.

The overwhelming heartbreak was visibly felt by the 30 or so people in attendance. What was nice was the comfort Lisa's dad gave her, including his ex-wife, which seemed to be as genuine as possible. He was obviously shaken by his daughter's, and her mother's, abject suffering, and found it within himself to do the right thing, which was noted by Ronnie and Lydia.

As well, Ronnie could imagine Lisa's father having his own moments of hard reflection, especially with regards to the three children he had brought into this world. How could one not?

Sometimes events like these seemed to close old wounds and Ronnie was hoping and praying for any kind of silver lining to be found with something so shocking. Time would tell. He would be faced with the unbelievable task of convincing Lisa that life was worth continuing, worth trying again and worth forgiving.

Lydia could feel the tension in her new husband's body and demeanor, and did what she could to alleviate Ronnie's pain, sometimes simply caressing his neck and gently squeezing.

There was no after-burial gathering, this was simply too much to continue and much too personal to intrude upon, good and noble intentions aside.

Ronnie spoke with Lisa, who was mildly medicated, her glassy stare bearing this.

"I will call you tomorrow, honey. Let your mom take care of you for now."

She gathered enough strength to hug her former guidance counselor fiercely, saying nothing, with Ronnie finally, and gently, breaking away, giving her back to her mom and dad.

Michael McBride approached Lydia and Ronnie, "Tough times, indeed."

He paused, and again spoke to Ronnie with evident love and respect, "Take tomorrow off, son. You need the rest. Lydia, maybe you can, too. He needs you now more than ever."

Both nodded in agreement.

Everyone left the cemetery, and Ronnie kept thinking about little Roman being left behind there. It started to depress him, but Lydia caught this immediately, and she took over with her words of faith, love and conviction.

Ronnie knew that he had the very best possible girl in the entire universe for him, and thanked God, once again, for their mutual destinies colliding.

That evening brought forth for the two of them yet another level of spiritual consciousness, and it was Lydia's words that allowed this to happen.

After pouring Ronnie a healthy tumbler of his favorite single malt scotch, she asked him to stretch out on their couch and listen to her, with his eyes closed.

He did.

She delivered, in a gorgeous, hushed tone, the most elegant soliloquy, he would ever know.

My darling husband, thank you for being in my life. When we first met, I knew you were special, but had no idea as to the depth and extent of the man I would come to know.

Just like you, I had my doubts as to where we were headed at times, but damn, were we physically right for each other.

This brought a quick smile to Ronnie's face.

But, we stayed the course, whatever that might have been, as now I'm finding it hard to even remember what it was like before we fell so hard for each other, and not that long ago, and I could clearly see in your actions and demeanor that you were exceptional.

You cared for your kids at school, and after you shared your college student's suicide with me, I knew even more so why you were placed in the path of so many adolescents. You were there to make a significant difference.

I could also see why you were placed in my path.

He started to say something, but Lydia's soft index finger on his lips quelled his action.

I watched you keep yourself in top physical and mental shape, and knew you worked so hard to do so. I often wondered why people, especially men, train in the manner you do, but life's recent events have educated me, greatly, and I thank you for your perseverance and dedication to the art you adore.

I can also see why your mentors, especially Master Ty and Principal McBride, love you so. They see themselves in you, clearly. It's that simple; and, as men of great respect, they, in turn, have found that in you, my darling Ronnie. You have earned their highest esteem, and I cannot tell you how wonderful that makes me feel.

I am so very proud of you, so very honored to be your wife, so very blessed to be in your life.

I do know this, our baby will have very best father this world has ever known...well, maybe you'll be tied with those angels that have proceeded us.

Again, Ronnie smiled at his wife's spiritual wisdom.

With the tragedy of Lisa and her little Roman, I also realized that I would have to share you with probably many, over the coming years, and I understand why.

God has blessed you, God has blessed me, and with that comes responsibilities to others that need love and guidance.

I don't want to share you, Ronin Maximus Van Valkenburg, the selfish side of me speaks to this, but, with my lovely name of Lydia Van Valkenburg comes the caveat of just exactly that, and I would not have it any other way.

Ronnie kept his eyes closed, took a sip of his scotch, and squeezed her hand.

I hope we have several babies, my darling and love of my life. I promise you that I will be the best mother ever, too. You can count on that. I cannot wait for our mutual souls being a part of our newborn baby. How magnificent will that be...

Don't forget, though, that I need you, too. I need you every night and every morning. I can live without seeing you all day, as long as I know we'll go to bed and awaken in each other's arms, forever.

Sleep Ronnie, right here, right now. I am not going to school tomorrow, so I'll be with you when you awaken, whenever that may be. Just let yourself float away, and take with you this kiss, and my eternal love and devotion. You've given me yours, now let me do the same, it's God's will.

Ronnie was asleep in seconds. Lydia's intuition and timing had been exactly what was required. He, like Lisa, would find peace only in sleep, and for quite some time, she feared.

What Lydia did not realize, however, was Ronnie's vast dreamscapes, and the tortuous rides they had become these last several months.

Thankfully, their Creator had a different plan that evening, and both Lisa and Ronnie found the respite sorely needed for internal repair, if for only a little while.

Lydia watched her husband sleep, and wondered how the two of them might survive something so tragic. At least they had each other, but still, it shook her up.

Poor Lisa did not have a husband or love to share the burden, not that she would want that, knowing how awful Bradley had been. Still, she was alone in a sense, even with her compassionate mother's love and care. It just was not the same.

Lydia went into their bedroom, just for a moment, to find one of her husband's treasured angel paintings, this one, his favorite, entitled "The First Kiss" by William Bouguereau.

The two very young angels, Psyche and Cupid, depicted in this famous work of art, spoke to Ronnie well beyond the normal scope of observation. This she knew, as he had often told her so.

They meant to him the power of God's will and the destiny for all, as a result thereof. They also gave him the sense of true love and those meant to be together in this life.

Lydia prayed for the strength to carry her baby to term, and the will to survive anything that might befall her husband and soon to be family. She realized that life was tough, but recent events had made her question her own veracity, which was absolutely normal. She knew this, but still had anxiety over all that had transpired.

Lydia so wished for a glass of wine, but quickly dispelled that irresponsible, albeit benign, thought, smiling at how beautiful their newborn would be and the ultimate love he or she would receive.

She gathered up the comforter on their bed and brought it into the living room and to the couch where Ronnie was soundly sleeping. Gently covering him, she let the other three-fourths fall to the floor, so she could slide the coffee table away and make room for herself, right beside and below the man she adored.

Pulling up a couple of pillows, she gave a last check on him, kissing him ever so lightly and saying, "I love you, Ronnie Vee, goodnight, baby."

She then lay down, pulling one of the pillows into her stomach, trying best to simulate her husband's body that she had become so used to, so secure by.

Lydia fell asleep, and thankfully did not dream, either.

XXVI

Lisa's counseling with Ronnie began in January, after the Christmas and New Year holidays had become a recent memory, and school had begun the proverbial dash to its late spring finish line.

During those vacation weeks, however, Lydia and Ronnie had taken most of that time to visit the Caribbean's beautiful Virgin Islands, once again. She had told him that while another destination would've been nice, and a new experience, she'd rather go to St. John, where they had previously stayed, as she was feeling quite nostalgic in her second month of pregnancy. Also, who knew if they'd make it back for quite some time as life was literally changing by the day.

It turned out to be a serendipitous choice in that several of the same hotel staff and island natives they had met there before were once again in their company, and the fact that they were now married with their first child on the way made it even more special for all involved and who had come to know this dynamic couple.

They had indeed made it another honeymoon, relaxing with the fact, whenever possible, that Lydia was carrying new life. She was the model for pre-natal care, and found that the numerous, alcohol-free cocktails created and provided for her by their most attentive staff were just wonderful.

They made love carefully, but with a new-found intensity that happens during pregnancy. Ronnie was overwhelmed by her passion and desire, with Lydia reminding him that "all was still well down there", and never without her intoxicating and electrifying smile.

They left St. John with a newfound sense of joy and purpose, leaving all who had interacted with them the promise of a return with their new baby, next year. Why not, they had thought. Why not expose their newborn to the world, and these new people even at what would then be four months of age?

Upon return home, reality set in quickly. Lisa was seriously damaged, as Ronnie could clearly see. He still had hope for her recovery, whatever that would be, but only if her progress showed more of a permanent effect as opposed to just a temporary fix. To him, that meant that she, in due time, must convince him of several key factors, small markers if you will, of things he had diligently researched for her specific paradigm.

Depression is vast, and to many people the very same events can have completely different outcomes, and entirely diverse reactions and manifestations. He also well knew that a suicide attempt once could readily mean another try again. He had to be extremely cautious with his young friend.

As well, Ronnie had Lisa start seeing his friend, the same woman that had been her therapist before when her parents were getting divorced during her senior year of high school, which seemed now like a long time ago. Also, this doctor could prescribe proper medication, when necessary.

They had agreed to meet in Ronnie's office, with the suggestion (and blessing) of principal McBride, every Monday, Wednesday and Friday, two hours before school let out. That way Lisa could come in and leave unnoticed after her one-hour session, and Ronnie would not lose precious time in his day, as he now had other obvious and new responsibilities.

Michael McBride understood the great capacity for compassion his young protégé possessed, but also knew that this could interfere with Ronnie's personal life, however important this undertaking was, and found a way to satisfy all involved. If a student required extra time with him, then, by God, they could find the time with their own schedules to meet with their guidance counselor superstar.

McBride now had a mission, too, besides being a high school administrator. This was to look out for Ronnie, when needed; someone had to, besides Lydia. He greatly appreciated this "big brother" role, and events time and again proved exactly so.

Both Michael and Ronnie had agreed that Lisa needed to get out of her house and away from all previous reminders of her tragedy, at least the tangible ones. Lisa's mom had also acquiesced with very little persuasion. Even though she wanted her mentally ravaged daughter close by, she knew she was in good hands with the men in her life that could be trusted and who loved her.

Miraculously, Lisa's father was showing as much support as possible, coming to spend time with his daughter a couple of times a week. Lisa was at first very non-receptive, but she could see that he was sincere and trying to reach her, and soon came to embrace her dad's efforts.

He had (of course) a new girlfriend, and, apparently, she was confident enough in herself to not be too jealous of this arrangement; perhaps she was one of the good ones, intelligent enough to understand that previous relationships, family, etc., all last forever, and that the events that had transpired were tragic enough to enlighten anyone.

This was the "silver lining" that Ronnie had hoped for...Lisa's dad trying to regain some semblance of that most important father-daughter paradigm that had proven over time to be so very important in all of our young girls' development, especially with regards to trusting the opposite sex.

Lisa's mother had no desire for a reconciliation, as well, she had "moved on" with her life and this manifested in a much needed, peaceful environment for all. The stars would have to align if Lisa was to survive basically intact, which was, of course, impossible, but still one had to hope for the best.

That first Monday back in school Ronnie heard a soft knock on his open office door, precisely at 1pm. Lisa looked a good ten years past her tender age of 20. This was to be expected, at least temporarily, but still Ronnie was a bit shocked. He did notice that she was clutching the Rosary he had given her, and was wearing the ring that Lydia had bought.

"Hi honey, it's so good to see you, come in," as he guided her to his ergonomically designed, reclining black leather chair, which he had expressly purchased for this very moment. In fact, Ronnie had described to the sales person at the high-end furniture store Lisa's exact size, hoping for a perfect fit. Why he had gone to this trouble, heaven only knows, but something had driven him to purposefully do everything in his power to make Lisa comfortable, even the simplicity of a nice chair.

"Hi Mr. Vee," was all she could manage at first. She was mildly sedated, but seemingly functional enough to interact.

However, she did ever-so-slightly smile, once seated, "Wow, this chair is nice, feels great..."

Her voice had trailed off into some vast and empty space, but at least it was a start.

Ronnie spoke softly, asking Lisa to just make herself as relaxed as possible, and to close her eyes, if she wanted; much the same as his wife had requested of him that previous evening. She made no visual objection or approval, for that matter.

Ronnie began, "I have thought about this moment for several weeks, Lisa, wondering if I could find the words to begin this path to our healing, and, yes, it is our healing; you and I are in this together, honey, never forget that."

"Life is so horribly cruel at times and this literally shakes whatever faith we have in God to the core; belief very often flies right out the window, as how could He be so unfair?"

Ronnie paused; Lisa was so relaxed he thought she might have already fallen asleep, but her slowly opening eyes proved contrary.

"You did the most magnificent thing, ever, in giving your son his chance at life, especially being so young yourself. Most girls, well, you know..."

Ronnie paused, taking a couple of deep breaths, he had to, as his mind was racing.

"I have thought so much about all of this, and how I came to love and appreciate you even more, for being so devoted to someone else. I always have been aware of your capacity for compassion, but this superseded everything."

Ronnie knew he had to be very careful here, especially when referencing, by name, her child. However, even though this belied certain "procedural methods", he took a chance.

"Baby Roman was your destiny, even for a little while here on earth, and I also feel that he will be your fate eternally. The mother that you became was nothing short of spectacular, and all could see this, especially me."

"Your mother and father, even separately, admired the strength and courage in their daughter. Principal McBride and Lydia were, as well, so impressed that they took the time to often say so to me. All of us were reminded of how much we could be capable of, and you honey, you were our collective example. We are all better for witnessing your adoration, love and commitment to Baby Roman, Lisa."

He paused again, knowing that that this was extremely painful, but at the same time Ronnie felt that any kind of communal appreciation and acknowledgment for her would lessen the despair of feeling alone. The fact that Lisa was seemingly comfortable and relatively sedate reassured him to continue.

"I know that you trust me, that's why you're here. I also know that you love me, and I do you. This is our common ground, Lisa, and ours to share. This will help you to heal, and everyone agrees, especially Lydia. She understands my purpose in life, and especially for you, and I cannot tell you how much this means to me."

Lisa opened her eyes again, and her faint but sad smile was more than enough to reassure Ronnie that he was, at least so far, on the right path in reaching this very precious and fragile young lady. More importantly, though, was the fact that she obviously believed his words and the direction in which they were leading.

They were both silent for a couple of minutes. Ronnie noticed that Lisa's eyes would widen, then narrow, and he attributed it to her medication and past glimpses of her baby's seven months of life with her. He could almost see her mind replaying events when her breathing would quicken and then diminish.

This was going to be tough, she was in so much pain and he was going to have to relive much of it with her if they were to evolve into some semblance of normal life again.

God, did he feel sorry for her and could not imagine himself in her shoes. He quickly said a prayer for Lydia and their yet unborn child. He brought his entire energy and focus back to Lisa, holding her hands and smiling. She then closed her eyes and fell asleep for the remainder of their first session.

As pre-arranged, Lisa's mother was waiting outside the high school and Ronnie escorted her to the passenger front seat, carefully placing her next to her remarkable mom and gently securing her seat belt.

Lisa abruptly pulled his arm next to her chest and held it there, not wanting to let go. Ronnie glanced at her mom whose tearing eyes, smile and slight nod gave him all the blessing he needed. He knew that they had been through hell in the last couple of years and he was honored to champion the cause of both women, who were becoming great friends to each other, as well.

One of the real reasons that Lydia loved him so and had committed her life to him was just this; Ronin Maximus Van Valkenburg had heart, and his capacity for honor and simply doing the right thing was never lost on her. Despite the shortcomings all of God's children possess, Ronnie was a good man, and the world was better for him.

He kissed Lisa on her cheek and bade them farewell. Their next session was just two days away, and Ronnie had some research to do, plus he was going to consult with Lisa's psychiatrist, knowing that while she could not share certain privileged information, their personal and professional friendship would allow her to help guide him into the right channels.

They both knew that ultimately Lisa's recovery would take a unified effort, and never was there a single doubt as to "client confidentiality". God was the absolute law for both these counselors, which is why Ronnie had suggested this amazing doctor for Lisa two years previous.

Watching them drive away hit Ronnie hard, and he suddenly lowered his head with tears in his eyes.

Principal McBride had observed Lisa's departure from his office window and was already on his way out, quickly walking to his younger friend who sensed his arrival but did not look up. Michael then cupped his hand around Ronnie's head and placed it on his shoulder, all the while scanning to see if anyone was approaching.

Fate had let them both have their privacy.

Ronnie then said to his mentor, "This is going to be hard."

Michael replied, "I know, son, I know."

After recounting with Lydia the day's events and eventually sharing a quiet yet romantic dinner, which found them kissing between nearly every bite, he was ready to crash. Lydia was too, as her pregnancy was draining her energy more and more.

Ronnie kept marveling to her his admiration for what had to be the toughest job in the world. She would just brush it off with her patented reply of "It's what women have been doing for all of time. I'm nothing special."

But in fact, Lydia was exceptional, and the reciprocal realization of their mutual benevolence was their bond, never to be questioned, attacked or shattered. They were two of the lucky ones.

Of course, Ronnie dreamed again. The hot bath and double martini assured him of a quick flight into his reverie. Had he known of what was in store, Ronnie might have forced himself to stay awake all night; however, life, unfortunately, doesn't work that way.

The two wolves had traveled south, following the Appalachian Trail into northern Georgia. It had been a long journey, but both were compelled to escape the harsh winter, which again belied normal behavior for this magnificent breed. Natural enemies were quite enough without having to literally freeze in a particularly harsh winter.

Maybe it was their age, they were getting on in years and had experienced quite a lot. But they had each other, and that was not lost on him, as every so often, he would point his snout to the sky and close his eyes in reverence, if only for a second or two. His raven mate had noticed him doing this but understood completely. That was their collective magic.

They had grown to completely rely on each other's perception of danger, and both were evolving into an almost singular mindset with regards to their individual needs, desires and survival skills.

The white wolf could sense that his mate had exorcised whatever demons she might have previously held, and this had helped him to find his own inner peace.

Still, they were in the wild and there was risk and peril everywhere. He just had hoped that his and her fighting days were behind them, but knew better; until death, no one was immune.

They now headed east, descending the Smoky Mountains and into the river valley that beckoned their call. The abundance of deer tracks assured them of an upcoming hunt and both were starting to feel the pangs of hunger.

As fate would have it, a singular young buck was nibbling grass at the river's edge. Normally, the wolves would have sought out a fawn or sickly adult, but none were in sight or smell. This was their prey.

He circled right and she left, with the cunning and stealth that only years of doing so would perfect.

They waited for several minutes, patiently letting the buck focus on his meal and momentarily letting his natural defenses perilously relax.

In a flash, he was on the deer biting at his legs and allowing his mate to go for the throat, both viciously trying to bring him down to the ground where they had a better chance at finishing, as he was young and strong.

The sound of an engine roaring shocked all three into a momentary lapse of action, allowing the buck to break away, freeing himself of his impending death.

The deer bounded towards the dirt road, adjacent to the river, then making a magnificent leap over it he was met in mid-air by the speeding all-terrain vehicle, both colliding in a sickening crash, killing him immediately and sending the driver head first into a tree, where her lifeless body now lay.

Normally they would've run away, but the white male and his raven mate crept up to the carnage. All was quiet, and they were shaken to the core. There had been too much human interaction lately, and this wasn't natural. She was so much more fearful than he, but that didn't stop either's compelling curiosity.

The raven wolf watched her white mate push the young woman's head gently with his nose, and then lick her face very carefully. She was confused by this, but trusted in his judgment and compassion. Again, crossing the natural line of human and animal, yet somehow understanding the sanctity of something beyond their power and control.

The alpha looked to the heavens and howled again. This mate soon joined in, creating a prayer for both souls recently departed.

Ronnie awakened and ever so carefully crept out of bed.

"What the fuck?" He again asked himself.

He was scared, and in a manner and fashion that was unknown to him. Having a person or two attack you placed immediate battle lines in the sand. This was easy, as it was a no-brainer. You fought for your life and those you love. Simple, easy, scary yes, but not confusing and certainly no doubt.

What was happening now, though, was beyond his control and expertise. It was "out of his hands", and this terrified him so.

He poured himself a tumbler of scotch and sat on their living room sofa. Drinking very patiently he was reminded by a college professor of his that he had adored; a Vietnam Veteran, two tours, who had once said to him, "Ronin Maximus Van Valkenburg, battle is easy, love is hard! One day you will know."

He now understood. Still, he prayed to be wrong.

XXVII

The ultrasound was stunning. There was life inside Lydia's beautiful belly, and this little baby was actually moving, with a very perceptible heartbeat, and all at roughly three months since conception.

Ronnie was so overwhelmed he started to lose it, but Lydia, knowing her husband so well, delicately pulled him to her face, compassionately letting him know this was their shared and miraculous destiny.

For the past several months his emotions were on full tilt boogie and it was truly wearing him out. God, was he spent.

Lately Ronnie had not been dreaming, and for this he was most thankful. There had been a few nights when he was so sure another fantasy would appear, but that had not happened. Still, he had not felt completely rested. He even got to the point of thinking about putting his personal training with Sifu DeAmbrosia off for a while, but his better judgment took over this thought…it was in his blood and the respite from his and Lydia's daily life was appreciated. Plus, a good workout and ass-kicking always did his psyche wonders.

Ronnie realized that he could re-evaluate everything after the baby arrived sometime in late July, but for now all was status quo. Sometimes, he feared the night and its potential to truly scare him. He thought about therapy, but there was simply not enough time at the present. For now, Master Ty would more than suffice, with his unique wisdom (hopefully) prevailing. Plus, his "older brother" Michael McBride would always be there for him; so, he too was in most capable hands, apart from Lydia's.

On their way, home they were both comfortably silent, much the same as many couples that are very secure with each other often find themselves...no need for banal dialogue. The impact of hearing and seeing their unborn baby was more than enough stimulation for the day. Still, they held hands, as always, and could physically feel each other's profound and dedicated love. How simply wonderful!

Lisa walked into his office on a rainy and cold, early February afternoon. Another eight or ten degrees lower and it would've been a major snow storm. Ronnie had that exact thought as he was never a fan of either cold weather or the blizzards that often accompanied and had often contemplated the thought of living by the ocean in a very warm part of the country, most likely Florida.

"Hi Mr. Vee, how are you today? I know you hate this kind of weather..." with an ever-so-slight slight smile.

This was a good sign. Lisa was initiating contact, and it was all so very important in her recovery. The fact that she was sharing something somewhat personal that they both already knew, was even better. Ronnie also noticed that she had actually made an attempt to look good...another significant indication. In fact, Lisa looked beautiful, and that filled his heart with love. He suspected that she was making headway with her psychiatrist, but her current demeanor was so welcome to him.

Recoveries of Lisa's nature often took years, and in many situations, there were never any real results of therapy, but occasionally a breakthrough was sudden, sometimes literally overnight, and Ronnie was hoping and praying for the best. Still, he realized there were miles to go.

"I drove here today," she added, which told him that she was not doing any medication. This was just great news. He knew she was extraordinary, but this was beyond anything he could've imagined, and made a mental note to share today's events with Lisa's doctor as soon as possible, although she might already have noticed, at least he had hoped so.

"Hi honey, you look gorgeous," and Ronnie's sincerity helped Lisa to an actual smile. "You cut your hair, it looks great."

"I've been wanting to for a while and just felt like doing something new..." as her voice trailed off.

This was yet another positive indication of her inner-healing, and Ronnie was nearly beside himself with hope for this still very young girl.

"Mr. Vee, your hair is nearly completely blonde, even white. I think it looks cool," which made him inwardly beam, even though she was stating the obvious. She was making small, but valiant attempts to engage him, and again, extremely positive demeanor on her part, which gladdened his heart.

She furthered, "My mom and I have gotten even closer, and I think that's because she was so afraid for me, possibly losing me."

Ronnie knew this was true. He was also aware that Lisa's recognition of the feelings of those, in this case, her mother, left in the wake of a suicide, and the exacting repercussions, was particularly paramount in anyone's absolute recovery from thoughts of taking his or her own life.

This was the most noteworthy breakthrough, for her. Now, he absolutely was going to call her doctor as soon as she left.

What he feared most, however, was that all of these encouraging signs from Lisa were much too early, but just what was "too early", anyhow? Ronnie possessed, sometimes to his detriment, the unique philosophy of "exceptional"; in other words, he forever had believed in a first time for everything, in all manners of life.

Someone had to start the ball rolling, and often he found himself doing exactly just that!

In this case, why not Lisa? Why not recover more quickly than "normal" (oh, how he disliked that word)? Maybe God had stepped in on this one...He had the ability, and Lisa had the strength.

Their session ended and Lisa's hug was probably too long, and too intimate, but Ronnie let it go. He knew that she loved Lydia and respected their marriage. Still, it made him wonder. However, he was not going to interfere with, unless necessary, Lisa's needs for any and all recovery moments.

Ronnie called her doctor, relating everything that had transpired, leaving out not a single detail, and they ended up talking for a good half hour. He was open to his friend's expertise, and welcomed her opinions, as they were in this together.

Conversely, Lisa's doctor knew that Ronnie was brilliant in his own manner and fashion, and this was due not just to his education, but more so to his intuitive acumen, and his ability to improvise with the life events of the myriad personalities he had dealt with over the years; especially that most precarious late teen to early 20's demographic that historically had been under extreme psychological and emotional attack.

"You've done well, Ronnie, truly Lisa is obviously in good hands. I sometimes think that I am much too "clinical" with my counseling, but that's my job, in a manner of speaking. I need to use the data that has mattered for years. The facts and methods that have been proven."

She paused, and then continued, "You, on the other hand, have this very special way to guide your patients, if you will, to find some sort of inner-strength and resolve based on their own processing. This, my good friend, is not found in any method book, nor can be taught by any university professor...and you and

I certainly share the same disdain for most of them," she added with a chuckle.

'Thank you, Heather," Ronnie responded, "I'm not sure what to say."

"There's no need to say anything, my dear. I always knew you were in exactly the right environment for making a difference in our kids' lives. And now, with Lisa, you matter even more."

Very high praise, indeed, coming from his psychiatrist friend that he respected beyond the norm.

He rhetorically replied, "Well, we still have our work cut out for us, do we not?"

And continued, "I am equally thankful for you taking charge of her. Obviously, she's better than she was, and that's all we can hope for."

"Yes, Ronnie, she is. Lisa's own decision to cut back on her medication, especially to drive to see you, is welcome news. She has been weaning herself, ever gradually, off of this last prescription. Yes, it was my suggestion, but it was her courage and willpower to do so."

She paused, and then concluded, "Let's still be cautious, Ronnie, but I know you realize that. Take care of her, and I will, too."

"God bless you, Heather, and thanks."

With that, they ended their conversation, and for the first time in months Ronnie felt the weight of the world lifted off of his shoulders.

He could not wait to relay to Lydia these recent events and his talk with Lisa's doctor. He knew that she was worried about him, and even though he had tried to hide most of his anguish, he knew better.

Lydia was one of the most intelligent and perceptive women

he had ever know, and sometimes one just knew that their true equal had been found, for better or worse. He realized, though, that this was for his enlightenment and had thanked God more than several times for her.

All of a sudden, he realized that school had been out for a while, totally losing track of time, and started down the hallway to leave, dialing Lydia on his cell phone.

"Hi honey, sorry it's late but I was on a call with Lisa's doctor, and we got caught up discussing the progress she was making, especially today, which was marvelous."

She replied, "That's great news, Ronnie, I cannot wait to hear about it later."

"I'm going to cancel my session with Sifu DeAmbrosia, tonight, I need to be with you..."

She cut him off, "No way are you doing that my beloved husband."

He let her continue, as he suspected what was coming.

"You need his coaching, and he needs you, too, if you've not realized this yet."

Lydia let Ronnie think about what she had just said, knowing that her husband's mental gears were turning.

He finally offered, "You're right, babe, I get it. I really do."

Ronnie could almost see his wife smile, knowing that she knew that he knew.

"I love you, Lydia, and I will forever."

"And I you, my dear, sweet Ronnie. Train hard and I will be waiting tonight with desire in my heart. We can make love and fall asleep...just the three of us," which made Ronnie laugh out loud.

God, he adored his wife and best friend.

Master Ty was in a particularly demonic mood this evening. Every once in a while, even he was subject to the will of life and its consequences. The warm-up stretching, forward and backward rolls, and then the break-falls and various jujutsu throws were an exercise in perseverance, to say the very least. Still, it was exactly what Ronnie wanted and needed.

Sifu ended this evening's session with some very hard-core, yet meticulous, gun defenses against multiple attackers, and Ronnie excelled, as usual.

De Ambrosia addressed his protégé, after the others had left the dojo, "Master Ronnie, very good training this evening. Your skills are becoming fine-tuned, but more importantly, your mind is calm and clear under duress, and this is where it matters the most."

Ronnie bowed his head in reverence, "Thank you Sifu De Ambrosia, I truly needed this workout tonight."

"I knew you did the minute you walked through the door."

He let that sink in before continuing, "How is young Lisa doing these days?"

Ronnie had not told Master Ty anything about the events surrounding Lisa's life, but word gets around, especially in the circles of friendship, communal love and compassion.

"She made a significant turn for the better today, and thank you for asking, Sifu."

"Ah, that's just fine news, my friend, fine news. You take care, and I will see you in two days. We are going to take our knife training to an even higher level."

This was welcome information to Ronnie, as the paradigm of the blade was his real expertise...for some reason it fascinated him to the point (no pun intended) of real insight and depth, psychologically speaking, as its use was so "personal". He also knew that most criminals carried them and the closer he remained with the most basic fundamentals and then the myriad of offensive and defensive techniques, far from novice, the better he felt.

He knew that the incident back in Frankfurt, Germany could have killed him, and he would always welcome Sifu DeAmbrosia's heightened training, and thank him.

On his ride home, he reflected upon the day's events and Lisa's seemingly miraculous recovery. He thanked God for the wonders in his life and his ability to help to heal those damaged souls that needed it most.

Again, he questioned the intentions of God and His design, as sometimes they were so very cruel. This was his personal dilemma, though, and he knew that quite possibly, no, quite probably, that he would never know. Still, he had faith when he "crossed over" that true enlightenment would spread her wings around his body and then, then would it all be so very clear.

For now, Ronnie just hoped for the best, as these tragedies of life were out of his control, which at times made him feel so helpless. Lydia and the baby were his focus, but that still brought him to tears at times, as the thoughts of anything going wrong, as in Lisa's case, literally ate away at his insides.

Still, he prayed for the strength to endure whatever came his way. What else could he do?

XXVIII

Winter slowly relented into spring, finally giving up her wicked cold, searing winds and wondrous snow falls to the early and often ambiguous warm currents of new life, fresh sounds and other welcome displays of our season of birth.

Lydia was more than half-way through her pregnancy and all signs were very good. Ronnie adored her so, now, even more than ever, and could not get over the fact that his wife seemed to be healthier, stronger and more vibrant than ever. As well, she simply got prettier, if that was even possible.

The senior students at his school seemed to collectively be on track for graduation and, for the first time that he could remember, there were no major personal issues with any of them. Strange and serendipitous all at once?

Ronnie wondered if this was by design. Did God actually lighten his load so as to focus on Lisa's recovery? He had a hard time believing so, as in the grand scheme of things, this was so very minor, but still, did He have a part in this? Ronnie's spiritual side believed possibly, yet his practical side countered that hope.

In the past, there were always cases of his students' home lives being turned upside down, or life-threatening illness, as with Jimmy McLaughlin's battle with leukemia and the magnificence of his will and perseverance. Ronnie would never forget this kid. How could he? Probably the most courageous events he ever witnessed, and not from just Jimmy, but his classmates, the high school faculty, administration and his immediate family.

Sometimes Ronnie wondered, as well, if he could continue with his vocation for much longer. It was very natural for counselors to get burned out, especially when the problems of those seemed to never end. But he always thought that he could handle anything. Now, Ronnie sometimes had his doubts.

His marriage, and now baby on the way, had changed everything, and while he realized that in life, life simply marches on, but at what cost? What else could he possibly do? More importantly, what would he even want to do other than his obvious "calling"?

Yes, his inheritance, at one time, was probably enough for himself to comfortably live, but not now; not with the responsibility of three lives, and who knows, maybe more.

That brief thought brought a momentary feeling of panic, but was quickly dispelled by thoughts of his incredible wife, and how she was maybe even tougher than he was. Actually, a few seconds more of said reflection told him that she most definitely was. He smiled to himself, which was always a good sign; this reaction he knew and trusted, implicitly.

Ronin Maximus Van Valkenburg was a true philosopher. He believed in the discipline and, more importantly, recognized the need for an acute awareness of its ever-changing tide. Life could always be explained; sometimes, though, it was not very pretty. Sometimes it was downright horrifying.

The psychology of the human spirit was also a very complicated paradigm. While logic seemed so easy at times, the thought processes of people, even with similar issues, could be so very different, and it was here that he excelled, at least so far.

His doctor friend Heather knew this, and had told him so, on more than one occasion. Ronnie's improvisational skills were unequalled, for the most part, and the myriad results spoke clearly for themselves, time and again.

Michael McBride evidently saw this, Sifu DeAmbrosia did so, too, but most importantly, his "patients/students" were the benefactors of the complete attention and focus of his heart and soul.

Yes, they were all patients, in a manner of speaking, each and every one of them. Gone was the norm of being just a faculty advisor to the student body. In its place was an environment of sanctuary, and an individual of real hope for those in desperate need.

Now, Lisa was coming in just once a week. Her recovery had been nothing short of miraculous, with both he and Lisa's doctor readily agreeing on less therapy in their respective offices and more healing to be found in Lisa's daily life and its encounters. She would sort it out, and she alone, with her faith in God, would be her necessary salvation.

Still, her once-a-week visits were anticipated by Ronnie, which both amused and scared him all at the same time. He knew this young girl was special, but why was she here in his life at this particular time, other than the obvious?

Especially since Ronnie had found the nerve, luck and timing to actually marry someone and start a family, something with which had previously never been more than a fleeting thought, and most certainly not his present endeavor.

He could not readily answer this, but it did not matter. Often, too much thought was too much heartache, confusion and paralyzing with its effects.

As usual, Lydia was home when he arrived. Since moving into their townhouse, which was almost equidistant from their respective high schools, but with hers being a little closer, she almost always arrived first. She had cut back on all extracurricular activities and responsibilities for the remainder of the year, due to her pregnancy, which was readily sanctioned by her principal; yet another administrator that had insight and compassion.

Lydia needed to be home, as soon as possible, after each day at work, mainly because she was tired. Her "mama bear" intuition guided her with all thoughts and actions these days, and preparing the nursery, for either a boy or girl, was her newfound passion.

"Hello, beautiful," Ronnie offered, coming through the front door. "How was school today."

She had grown to look forward to her husband's brief, yet anticipated greeting and, even though its deviations were minor, it was something she cherished, as his intentions were true to heart. What could be greater?

"Come here and kiss me, you gorgeous man," her very own usual reply, and equally coveted by Ronnie.

They both decided on an early dinner, after dragging him into their bedroom for a quick and intense sexual encounter.

Again, Ronnie was mystified by her desires, especially with her belly growing by the minute and knowing she was exhausted, quite often, these days.

He was, however, perceptive enough to go with her flow, knowing that she knew...it was truly that simple, and he welcomed this relief from everything outside of just them.

Both went to bed earlier than usual.

Ronnie dreamed, again...

The two wolves found themselves migrating back up to the Blue Ridge Mountains of Virginia, as the weather's changing tide signified the advent of spring. Their thick undercoats were shedding and both looked a bit patchy, almost mangy; however, these two alphas and their general countenance would belie any sense of perceptive letdown to any eyes laid upon them, human or otherwise.

The last encounter with the dead girl changed both of them, once again. Their natural fear of the human race was becoming something entirely else, and neither tried to figure it out anymore.

The white and raven mates were in a transformation of sorts, and only God knew this unique plan. Their love for one another had grown and grown, with each passing event, and each passing day.

They frolicked in the warm sun of early spring, whenever possible and when predators were nowhere to be heard, smelled or seen. The white wolf seemed preoccupied with constant moving, as if a destination was already planned, and his mate respected his intuitive focus, with both eventually coming out of the safety of the mountains and finding themselves traversing the farmlands of central Northern, Virginia, but only at night.

Ronnie could feel an undeniable compression in his chest and an aching in his guts. Both sensations, however, were more calming than agitating, almost as if his vital signs were being monitored by a physician that he trusted and a nurse so pretty that if he died then and there, his last vision would be worthwhile.

The wolves were headed to him, he knew this now. He also now believed that the white wolf, in particular, already having appeared in some of his previous reveries, was trying to communicate with him.

Why? Again, only God could know, but his dream was more vivid than ever before; hell, it was now a reality.

Ronnie tried to wake himself, but could not, feeling paralyzed in his sleep. He hated this feeling and it was the subject of more than a few nightmares, but somehow this was different, not quite so distressing. Maybe a guardian angel was in play...maybe two!

He finally broke the bonds of his restraint and sleepwalked, or floated, to his bedroom window. At least he thought he did.

The silvery moonlit night, and howling wind, was the perfect backdrop for what he would never forget.

The white wolf of his dreams was standing there, fur blowing with each gust, and staring straight at him, into him, without malevolence, but with compassion and understanding. The magnificent beast's eyes were transfixed in a manner that touched his heart and caressed his soul.

His raven mate was stunning, not only in beauty, but in her countenance, which belied anything but subservient; almost the male's size and black as coal. Her head was firmly buried into her mate's, not even glancing up at Ronnie.

Lisa, dreamed, as well.

She crept up to the edge of the woods, standing there watching, without sound and movement, remaining in the shadows as to not alert and frighten them.

Two very young humans were frolicking in the pastoral meadow, seemingly without a care in the world, laughing and somersaulting, and just being...well, boys!

Summer was in full swing and the world's cares and woes oblivious to them, as it should be.

Lisa was very content, continuing to watch their antics and play, marveling at how life could be so much fun, and so profound in its simplicity.

She wondered where her white mate exactly was at the moment, having wandered off from him a few minutes ago; yet, she suspected that he, too, was watching these boys, understanding the connections involved.

Lisa enjoyed being a magnificent alpha female, and the freedom from human life, even though it was only at night and on rare occasions. She was, without arrogance, very proud of her raven hued coat and hazel eyes, but mostly she knew she was different, and could see this clearly in her mate's eyes. His respect and love was clear, that she knew, and that she cherished.

She felt his presence next to her, and they both continued to watch these two kids play for a good while. They both understood the significance of what was happening, and its message from God letting them know everyone was fine.

Ronnie awakened the next morning, as usual finding Lydia already up and about, getting prepared for her, and his, day at school.

Her energy and passion for life was something to behold, and something to be respected at the highest level.

The smell of coffee, just brewed for him, gladdened his heart, further sanctifying her extremely unselfish behavior. She was going to be a magnificent mother. He only hoped and prayed to be half as good a father.

He would not reveal his previous night's fantasy. He could not.

Ronnie's sense of confusion and trepidation was becoming too much of a distraction to just dismiss, but dismiss he exactly did, saying fuck-all to the gods of dreams and whomever else was in power at the present time. Fuck all of them and the horses they rode in on!

This empowered him, helping to pave the path in feeling whole and confident, once again.

It was raining, yet he insisted, as his etiquette always dictated, on walking Lydia to her car, holding the umbrella over her, and not him. She never took this for granted, however, always telling herself that Ronnie was the one.

His caressing and kissing her before getting in was their model, but this time, just maybe just a little too passionately, a little too longingly, caused her to step back, look at him and comment, "Wow, honey, are you alright?"

He knew that he had betrayed his innermost thoughts, but quickly composed himself and replied, "Yes, babe, it's just that I find myself falling in love with you, constantly," letting his voice decrescendo.

"Your eyes just mesmerize me, and I cannot help it."

This prompted Lydia to put her things in the front seat of her car, and then, facing her beloved husband, say, "You are my world, Ronin Maximus Van Valkenburg, never, ever doubt that."

Pausing, and further adding, "God brought you to me, and me to you. For whatever reason, for whatever plan, He needed us to do this," opening her arms, in a gorgeous display of compassion, faith and promise.

Ronnie was so close to crying that he couldn't stand it. Somehow Lydia knew and just pulled his head into her shoulder, embracing and, at the same time, letting him know how tough he truly was.

Both understood each other, completely.

Isn't this what it's all about?

He stood there, waving goodbye and getting soaked, but it did not matter. He had fallen in love all over again.

Lydia sounded her horn, and waved back, with her left hand's palm facing him, as her custom, fingers displaying in their sublime and individual mini-dance.

He could almost see her smile, even a quarter mile away.

❦ ❦ ❦

It was the very last time Ronnie would see his beloved wife, Lydia Van Valkenburg, and he would never know his child.

The coroner's report revealed instantaneous death upon

impact, for both Lydia and her baby, her car being hit by a tractor trailer, whose brakes had apparently locked up due to the intense rain, squealing through an intersection, just blocks from her school.

The driver had also died.

The news was delivered to Ronnie that morning by his friend Michael McBride. As fate would have it, Lisa's weekly session was in progress, having been moved to the morning to free him up for a parent conference later, that afternoon.

The knock on Ronnie's office door immediately alarmed him. His principal walked in with tears in his eyes.

Lisa knew.

Ronnie knew.

He fainted into Lisa's and Michael's arms, both laying him on his couch.

Ronnie woke in his hospital room, two days later.

Sifu De Ambrosia, Michael McBride, Lisa and her mother were all there, as were his two sisters Vanessa and Valerie.

In his right hand was the rosary given to Lisa by him, when she had needed it most.

Seeing everyone, Ronnie immediately knew that all that had happened was real.

He squeezed his right hand, closed his eyes and most mercifully fell asleep.

XXIX

Lydia's funeral was a very small and private affair, as Ronnie, and his sisters who orchestrated the entire ceremony, could not fathom the multitude of sorrow emanating from his and her current and former high school students and administrative associates.

Their immediate families and extremely close friends were more than enough to help bear the impossible grief. Lisa and her mother and father had attended, as well; Lisa's dad knew exactly what Ronnie had done for the recovery of his daughter.

Even though he was heavily medicated by normal standards, he knew where to draw the line with the pain-killer script his doctor and good friend had sagely advised, as Ronnie had found himself in the depths of an abyss where he could never had imagined, and his doc could read this all too clearly.

Lydia's and their unborn baby's cremated remains were ceremoniously blessed and given to Ronnie's sisters to hold for him, until that time when he could give her back to the sea they both loved and adored.

Vanessa and Valerie also, and in record time, had commissioned a well-regarded craftsman to create for this occasion an ornate, yet in no way ostentatious, bench of iron and deep red mahogany, to be placed in the local cemetery by the pond, where one could find respite in just sitting down, relieving themselves, if only for a moment, of the intolerable burdens weighing heavily upon beaten shoulders.

Lydia would've loved this simple gesture, Ronnie's sisters had no doubt.

In the middle of this hallowed bench's iron scrolled backing was the letter "L" sitting inside of the letter "V", silver in color and raised upon a modest pewter plaque, solidly embedded to remain there for all of eternity.

At the end of the service Michael McBride returned Ronnie to his house; it's where he wanted to go. He, along with Ty DeAmbrosia, Vanessa and Valerie and a few others, had all offered their homes, or to stay with Ronnie at his, but he wanted to be alone, he needed to be alone, he had to be alone.

He had convinced all, especially his sisters, that he would be fine. Still, they had never seen their younger brother in such a state of despair and were worried, understandably.

Lisa knew better, though. She drove to his house, after everyone had left, knocked on his door and said, in no uncertain terms, "I'm sleeping on the couch tonight, and I don't care what you think, say or do, I'm going to be here when you try to take yourself out, Ronnie Vee; I know you, and fuck you if you disagree. I'm not losing both of the boys that truly saved me!"

He knew she was referring to her baby Roman, as well as him, and it cut through him like a razor-sharp blade.

That was that.

This simple, defiant and prescient gesture saved the life of Ronin Maximus Van Valkenburg that night. It was that simple, and it was that true. No amount of counseling could've brought Ronnie to any sort of clarity, at least in the next few months.

Lisa had disclosed her intentions to Michael and Ty, as they both had discussed staying with him that night.

McBride told her that he would be available at any time, should she need him.

The first thing Lisa did, when she entered Ronnie's house, was to go straight to his bedroom's dresser, where his wedding picture with Lydia stood, and grab the bottle of pain-killers that were right beside it. God only knew how she had known where to find them, but find them she did.

She would give him one, and then another, duly spaced out and with no martini or scotch kick start, only water. It was time to clean up, and it started this evening, with all medication paced carefully, and just the proper amount of love and understanding.

So, Lisa absolutely knew.

Ronnie knew she knew, as he had taught her well.

Heather, Lisa's doctor and his friend, also knew, and was right by Lisa's side, if only metaphorically, at least for now.

The white and raven alpha wolves also knew. Their howls of prayer for their human spiritual connection were heard for miles and miles.

God knew...just because.

XXX

Life has its own manner of revealing itself, to all that enter this sacred world, and to all that inevitably leave.

Some experience this without extreme highs and devastating lows, and many times that is not just serendipitous but a matter of choice, at least with regards to chosen mates, vocational choices, places one lives, travel destinations, etc. Countless are satisfied with this, to more or less stay the course, as it's much easier on the psyche and soul, not to mention the blood pressure. Nothing wrong with this, just that a course of action such as this was not even a small part of Ronnie's vocabulary.

The halcyon days of Ronin Maximus Van Valkenburg were gone, not that his path was ever that tranquil, but now, now life was vastly different. His remaining days would be an exercise in coping and survival, plainly and simply.

Many believe that we are handed our fate, if one can reason and abide by this philosophical impression. Others feel we create our own singular destiny. Probably, the truth lies somewhere in between.

Still, one doesn't have to always like it, or accept its determinations.

Ronnie was scarred beyond comprehension, and those that knew him well, and loved him even more, knew it too.

These last two-plus weeks, post Lydia's funeral, were a continuous dream, conscious or not. Michael McBride, Ty DeAmbrosia, Vanessa and Valerie had all stopped in to see him.

Even Lisa's mom came by a couple of times, but make no mistake, she also was there to make sure her daughter was okay, as Lisa had not left Ronnie's side for the entire time.

She had camped out in the living room, as it was the proper place to be in his townhouse, minding to herself but being available for the nightmares that plagued her beloved mentor literally every single night.

She also had cooked all their meals, and was there to coerce Ronnie into eating, and taking a shower or a bath every other day...if only to just feel the hot water's mercy upon his soul.

Lisa also was maintaining his pain killers. She had mathematically and creatively, with the advice of her doctor Heather's and Ronnie's personal physician, figured a schedule whereby he would be free of them within the next six to eight weeks. All were on the same page. All wanted the same thing for him.

She recognized that he was ever-so-gradually improving, even if others did not, as the terrifying reveries ceased three nights ago. For those glorious and sacred evenings Ronnie slept peacefully. Lisa could read the small signs, those microcosmic events that only someone that knew, would know.

She felt that his eyes were enough information to gauge his recovery, and if salvation was even possible.

She prayed for Lydia's and her baby's souls, and she prayed for Roman's. All she asked of God was peace for Ronnie, and continued enlightenment for herself. This wasn't too much to request, and if it was, well then fuck all.

Even if Ronnie didn't realize it yet, he would soon enough...he was the white alpha and she the raven, and the universal design of all that had happened was now as clear as it could be.

She knew that he did not have to dream of wolves anymore. Neither did she.

Lisa only hoped that life would somewhat disclose itself, at least with regards to pain and suffering. She knew that the world had experienced infinite examples of tragedy, but where was the logic?

Where was the end-game to all of this?

Why would God subject anyone to this level of heartbreak?

One particular afternoon, while Ronnie was napping, she sat cross-legged in the middle of the living room and meditated, as her doctor and Ronnie had taught. With the sun's warm rays caressing her face, she breathed slowly, very deeply, and with a calmness that belied anything she knew.

Lisa's thoughts wandered and then gradually started to dissipate, eventually progressing to a singular white dot, holding that image for quite a while. This tiny, yet intense, circle started to evolve into a shape, that of Jesus Christ. Her mind then started to evoke whatever her conscious and sub-conscious memories possessed, regarding what she knew of His life and death. She concentrated like never before, tuning the rest of the world completely out.

Lisa tried to imagine God's grief of watching His Beloved Son being nailed to the cross. She placed herself into His Mother Mary's observing eyes and soul, assimilating into Her entire body. Clearly realizing Mary's utter pain and total anguish, with her own body starting to shake, Lisa shouted "Oh, no," and then fainted, collapsing sideways and falling gently into her guardian angel's arms.

Ronnie held her there for a moment, letting her breathing restore to some semblance of normal, and then lifted her onto the couch, covering her with a blanket. He sat across from her, closing his eyes, only after knowing she was alright.

He was spent, precipitating another dream, but this time it was beautiful, this time it was just, this time it was deserved...

Lydia held his hand and walked him into the cemetery's garden, where they both sat on the bench his sisters had so thoughtfully provided.

No one said a word for several minutes, as they both tried to comprehend the hand that life had dealt them.

She spoke first, "Honey, we are fine, please believe me. Look into my eyes, there you will see the truth for yourself."

Ronnie understood that "we" meant Lydia and their unborn baby boy. His throat clutched, causing him to nearly hyperventilate, but Lydia's hand reassured that he would be alright.

She continued, as Ronnie could find no thoughts or words or any manner of expression. He felt paralyzed, but actually calm.

"For us, it will be but a blink of an eye when we see you again. You will live whatever years you have. Live them well, my love, please live them well, whatever transpires. Follow you heart, your dreams, your instincts. I know what is inside of you, my soul mate, and I truly recognize the capacity for love you possess. I also appreciate and greatly admire your sense of duty, of right and wrong."

She paused, and then added, "God loves you, too."

Ronnie was heart-broken yet mesmerized all at the same time. He wanted Lydia so badly, but knew that he would have to wait.

"I just wanted to die, and then I'd be with you, honey."

Lydia smiled at him, "I know, babe, I know. You need to finish your purpose, your truth. The magnificence of your capacity to heal is so important to so many, Ronnie. Be there for them, and guide those that seem to have no way out to realize the truth and wonder of their existence. Help them, honey. Save as many as you can."

They held hands for quite a while, with Ronnie looking directly into Lydia's eyes. He closed his own, falling momentarily asleep, and when he awoke, he was holding Lisa's hands, looking into her eyes and understood completely.

Lying beside each of them, at their feet, were the two Alpha wolves, almost as if they were there for protection, but Ronnie knew better...they were there for love and affection and the meaning of everything that had transpired.

Ronnie opened his eyes slowly, almost afraid of whatever vision might lay before him. Lisa was still fast asleep on his couch, and the afternoon sun was starting to slip away.

This gave him a sense of calm so desperately needed that it could only be Divine Intervention. There simply had not been enough time to heal from events so horribly tragic, yet here he was, feeling alright and breathing normally.

He slipped into his bedroom, so as not to disturb Lisa, and quietly called Michael McBride.

"Hello Ronnie, are you okay?" was his immediately response.

"Yes, Michael, I'm fine, and I need to see you, but it can wait until tomorrow."

"I can be there in 20 minutes, my good friend," he answered, with a touch of urgency in his voice.

"No need to. I promise you that I feel better, and I want you to see me in person...so you will know, too. I want you to see for yourself, to look directly at me. I could never hide any truth from you, and I know that you can appreciate that."

These last words from Ronnie brought an audible sigh of relief from Michael. If there was one thing that anyone on earth could count on, it was the conviction of Ronin Maximus Van Valkenburg.

"Shall I drive by tomorrow morning, on my way to school?"

"No need to, Michael. Anyhow, you know that I'm not on your

way to school, but thanks for the offer. I will slip into your office after the first bell. Plus, I need to gather some things from my office."

He paused, and then added, "I realize you will probably ask me to take the next year off, but I will argue with you until I convince you otherwise. These last remaining weeks will be quite enough leave of absence for me. Please trust me on this, Michael. My purpose in this life is right there in our high school. Our kids, my beloved big brother, yours and mine. This is God's plan and you know this, all too well and all too clearly."

"Well then Ronnie, I shall look forward to giving you one of my bone-crushing hugs, and just maybe a kiss, from this big ol' Irish son-of-a-bitch."

That made Ronnie smile.

He then called Sifu DeAmbrosia and his sisters Vanessa and Valerie, spending just a few minutes with each, but enough time to know that they knew.

Time would, of course, prove a better version of himself, but for now this would have to suffice.

He saved the last call for Lisa's mom, thanking her for her daughter's care and love, assuring her that she was peacefully asleep on his couch.

Ronnie could tell from where a great part of Lisa's character came, and let her mom know so.

He thought about his dream, and felt lucky to have spent those few precious moments with Lydia. He knew greater forces were in play and did not question them. Perhaps life would continue to reveal itself, perhaps not. He, however, strongly felt the former.

Peeking in on Lisa revealed that she was in an extremely deep sleep, as the extra blanket he put on her elicited nothing more than a beautifully soft sigh.

She seemed at genuine peace. He thanked God. It was likely she, too, had experienced a vision like his, and was slowly processing her very own means of coping, survival and path to continue living.

He hoped so. She was much too wonderful a cosmic spirit to burn out before her time. Her essence would be the caressing light of many souls in her future, and quite possibly his.

Ronnie licked his thumb and lightly, ever-so-discreetly, drew a cross on her exposed cheek.

She did not move, but he could detect the slightest smile with the corner of her mouth.

Ronnie felt his Father, His Son and The Holy Spirit.

XXXI

That late summer, Ronnie opened a letter from Lisa's mom, delivered by Federal Express. Inside was a copy of an internet story about Bradley's arrest and pending hearing. There had not been any contact with or mention of him since Ronnie had "educated" him and his three friends that particular day outside of the wine shop, where their ill-fated attack had taken place.

Bradley was accused of attempted rape and 1st degree assault of a young woman, who was attending the same college.

She had been severely beaten, with facial and body lacerations that showed direct and very compelling evidence of rage and humiliation.

The fact that he was out on bail belied every sense of trust in the judicial system Ronnie possessed, but he knew why...age old story of money and power.

Lisa had resumed living with her mother, but had found herself visiting Ronnie nearly every single day. Sometimes they shared a meal, sometimes they took long walks and just talked, but that was the extent of their relationship; two beautifully connected best friends, and it felt good for both of them.

He showed Lisa the letter, knowing that her mom had sent it to him so he would make that decision, not her.

Lisa sat silent for a minute, processing all of this.

She looked at Ronnie and gave him her open palms, so that he would place his in hers.

She looked into his eyes, "It's time to end this, Ronnie."

It was as declarative a statement as could possibly have been made, by this seemingly benign young lady.

As well, her former sobriquet, "Mr. Vee," had vanished by now. They had been subjected to more than enough tragedy for formality anymore. Plus, the relationship they now shared was beyond special. Ronnie and Lisa had become best friends, and they both needed and realized this.

Lisa had once told him, when she had finally felt like giving life another chance, after her son's death, that Ronnie's smile and his compassionate eyes seemed to cancel any sort of nightmare that she sensed was in the immediate queue. Ronnie now realized exactly the same truth for him. The magic of empathetic reciprocity from loving souls was crystal clear.

As for the revenge factor, it was certainly on both of their minds, but something else was at play here...more of an "animal purpose", where nature took its instinctive course, and not necessarily the cold-blooded calculations of the human mind. Most likely, once again, it was something in between.

The blackness Ronnie had felt in his heart, after losing Lydia and their baby, now had a purpose apart from the one that wanted to destroy him.

The metamorphosis of Lisa and he and the Alpha wolves was progressing, and now very evident. This due to the malevolence and arrogance of a young man who had always gotten his way his entire life, with no real repercussions other than that one good beating from Ronin Maximus Van Valkenburg, which apparently hadn't been enough of a life-lesson for this predator.

Bradley and his friends that day had re-written that incident into their own explicable chapter that would become revisionist, self-flattering history.

Now, however, and unknown to him, he was prey.

XXXII

The crystalline night sky was perfectly sublime, and even though the temperature of 28° was unusually warm this December night, the air could still cut you like a knife with its bone-chilling winds whipping violently off of the ice.

Deep Creek Lake, in Western Maryland, was the summer and winter playground for thousands every year. With its 69 miles of shoreline, and Wisp Mountain and ski resort just a half mile away, this recreational paradise offered one of nature's finest destinations.

The felony rape and assault charges against Bradley had been reduced to criminal endangerment and simple assault, due to an obviously dedicated and well-funded effort on the part of his family and their battery of attorneys; and, almost assuredly, a not-so-small amount of money to the victim and her family.

Once again, this sociopath was free and clear of any kind of punishment, and moral conscience. History has shown, in cases such as these, that eventual escalation, which was always promised, sometimes resulted in the deaths of young women.

Bradley, home on Christmas break, had decided, along with his parents, that it was prudent to get out of town for a while, as the negative press from the diminished allegations was still fairly recent. His mother and father had suggested and, of course, paid for an extended weekend stay in one of the more secluded Swallow Falls Cabins, knowing that the chances of anyone seeing him were pretty much non-existent.

As all things strange, he had convinced yet another girlfriend of his to meet him there the day following his Friday afternoon arrival.

Bradley, along with a couple of his lacrosse buddies, had recently progressed heavily into cocaine, and, together with a couple of grams, he had also brought his favorite tequila and a case of Rolling Rock beer.

One night alone would be fine, as he could get trashed, watch a movie, and decompress from the madness with which he'd been involved, albeit it his own fault. Then, with Tiffany arriving early the next afternoon, he could shower and sober up in time for the myriad of sexual activities he had planned for this hot and ambitious, yet naïve, young woman.

He thought to himself, smirking, "They were all clueless, stupid and weak, just asking for it. Fucking bitches, every one of them."

He had also occasionally reflected of his own mother in exactly the same fashion.

❮ ❮ ❮

Ronnie sold his townhouse. He had to. Too many reminders of Lydia and what their lives had been. He was currently living in a rented A-frame condo that backed up to the Catoctin Mountains, a few miles west of where he was previously.

Michael McBride had met with him just two weeks before school was supposed to start, and during that discussion had strongly suggested Ronnie take a year's leave of absence, quietly saying, "Son, your job will always be here for you, and so will I. That's a promise."

This had brought a wetness to his eyes that were by now way

past the point of crying, even though they were still endeavoring their level best.

Ronnie had agreed, as something inside was clearly compelling him to follow the advice of McBride's, or really anyone he trusted other than himself, for that matter. Michael, though, was the perfect choice for this particular counsel, in that Ronnie's profound love, honor and respect for his friend was unquestioned.

He had also sold his beloved Porsche. Again, too many remembrances of the times he and Lydia had shared traveling together, screaming down the highway and taking curves as if they were on a race track, feeling the tightness of its suspension gripping the road and vibrating their bodies.

He now drove a black, four-door Jeep, and had actually gotten used to the complete difference in vehicles rather quickly. Maybe because he was in a totally different "place" these days; he had changed, understandably and undeniably, and knew that he was continuing to evolve into what only God could possibly know.

Lisa had helped him pack his things and move, and the company she provided was more than welcomed. She kept him focused when he showed glimpses of painful regression, and knew how to make him smile and sometimes even laugh, once again.

It was also Lisa that had found his current condo, persuading him to just rent for a while, and the fact that this local mountain range was within grasp was not so coincidental.

She knew of the conversion that was taking place, even if Ronnie had only suspected so. The Alpha male and female were a part of their existence, in dream and reality.

❦ ❦ ❦

The waning crescent moon cast just enough reflected light from the snow to create seemingly living and breathing shadows everywhere. A mountain lion's cry cut through the region, reminding everyone that this was her turf that night, or at least it used to be.

They pulled up to a very isolated spot, at the end of a small road, maybe a mile from the cabins. Ronnie and Lisa quietly got out and opened the tailgate of his Jeep, freeing the white male and his raven mate to explore this new terrain. The wolves had been extremely cooperative on the four-hour drive, almost as if they were in a pre-battle meditation.

If anyone had witnessed this, especially from a distance, it would've appeared to just be two large dogs getting out to stretch their legs and mark new territory.

However, this was around midnight and no one had seen anything.

After they had vanished into the trees, Lisa and Ronnie waited another ten minutes or so. He then poured each of them one shot of an extremely expensive single malt scotch he had brought, just for ceremonial purpose and sanctity. The toasted their beloved Alphas with a gentle touching of their glasses and a very benign kiss. They then made the long drive home, without a word being said, feeling a satisfaction that was transcendent.

That night they slept together for the very first time. No sex, just the comfort of two souls that needed the miracle of connection and warmth.

Both experienced a respite in sleep that had vanished, yet now returned to remind them of the possibilities of healing.

XXXIII

The two magnificent wolves crept up to the cabin, ever so cautiously, and waited, out of sight, by the trees.

Bradley, after consuming several beers and lines of cocaine, amidst shots of tequila, was trashed beyond previous experience. Knowing this, he had added one more fat line for "clarity".

The sexually explicit movie he had watched left him feeling like he wanted to masturbate but he knew that he couldn't. He would just have to wait for Tiffany, the next day.

He needed some air and decided to make use of the seclusion and piss outside, in the wilderness, like men did when they had the opportunity in this environment, like his dad would've insisted, like his dad always demanded.

He staggered to the edge of the front deck, reeling from being so wasted, suddenly feeling the temperature's piercing edge, yet forcing himself to finish what he had begun.

He started ever so slowly, then finally flowed with his much-needed relief. He heard a small scraping sound and became immediately alert, zipping up as quickly as possible, under the circumstances.

"Who's out there," he shouted to no one in particular.

Silence.

Walking to the other side of the porch, he stood there and just listened, long enough to satisfy his fear that it was just the winds howling; except, the howls were getting louder, completely confusing him.

Materializing before his very eyes were two monsters, white and black, their blazing eyes burning holes into his very soul.

Bradley was paralyzed, his heart starting to race like the wind surrounding him.

These two creatures just stared, motionless, almost as if they wanted him to think about dying, before it actually transpired.

The white and raven wolves then simultaneously snarled, so viciously and deep-throated as to be heard throughout the entire region, sending their message of redemption to all that needed this most profound lesson in life.

Bradley backed up, his heart exploding while tripping and hitting his head on one of the wooden beams supporting the upper-level deck.

The Alpha wolves vanished into their surrounding habitat, home at long last.

EPILOGUE

Exactly one week later, Lisa's mom had emailed Ronnie something she had found on a local internet news site.

She knew he would show it to her daughter, as Lisa had stayed with Ronnie the entire time, which was without any repercussion, whatsoever, from either her or Lisa's brother and sister, or even her former husband.

In fact, she had never felt better for the well-being and support of her daughter as she did now. She trusted, respected and loved Ronnie, implicitly, as she should.

She also, and more importantly, knew that Lisa's love for Ronin Maximus Van Valkenburg was unconditional.

It read:

Authorities are still looking into the death of a local young man who was found outside his rented cabin, at the Deep Creek Lake resort in Western, MD., last weekend.

A young woman, who remains anonymous, had traveled there to visit him, finding his body on the front deck upon arrival, whereby she immediately called the local police.

The preliminary autopsy report said, "Heart attack, and blunt force trauma to the brain, both brought on by an excessive amount of cocaine found in the bloodstream and the obvious indentation found on his skull, matching exactly a wooden supporting beam."

Ronnie knew that this was Bradley, but how did Lisa's mom make the connection as no name was given in the press?

Still, like her daughter, she was resourceful and prescient, and dedicated enough to find applicable justice, wherever it chose to present itself.

Word would get out soon enough. The only reason "the authorities were still looking into it" was that Bradley's parents were not accepting the obvious facts, and believed, from experience, that nothing was ever their own fault.

The article continued:

Also found just outside the cabin were many animal tracks, but undetermined, as the rains that morning had washed them nearly completely away, leaving only speculation as to their origin. One theory was that they might have been the prints of a wolf or two, but since none of these animals had been spotted in this region for several years, this particular connection was immediately dispelled by a local Park Ranger.

That night, Lisa and Ronnie found themselves giving their bodies to each other, cautiously, but with the determination of the creatures they had become.

Both had very quietly cried immediately after, but with these particular tears being the absolute catharsis of the collective tragedies that had fallen upon them these last couple of years, and the reprieve they had granted two souls deserving of another chance at life, whatever that would entail.

They embraced for what seemed an eternity, losing track of time and space.

Ronnie said it first, "I love you, honey, always have and always will."

Lisa smiled with her gorgeous and adoring hazel eyes, letting him know exactly the same.

He furthered, "Stay with me…forever."

There was no need for any reply.

Both had evolved into Alpha mates, just like their animal counterparts…a parallel marvel if ever there was. Both pairs suffering God's directives, yet somehow finding the way to spiritual enlightenment, albeit nearly killing each in the process.

❦ ❦ ❦

Ronin Maximus Van Valkenburg would marry Lisa the following year, with the blessing of his beloved Lydia, who appeared in his dreams one last time for this very particular reason.

There would be no public ceremony, and no official verification of this. Only the two of them sitting on Lydia's memorial bench in the cemetery, with each gently placing on the other's hand a simple gold wedding band, one having a dark, almost raven hue and the other a white tone, pledging faith and trust for their remaining days, here and in God's eventual, holy realm.

As well, both had Lydia's jeweler, the same one that had made her engagement ring, and Lisa's gift from them, create matching crosses to complement their wedding bands. Simple, yet spiritually elegant in look and design.

When commissioned for this task, he had burst into tears, knowing too well of everything they had gone through, and insisted on accepting absolutely no payment. This was his "needed blessing and honor", as he had eloquently declared.

Ronnie and Lisa had most graciously accepted his generosity and benediction. Both had kissed him.

Ronin Maximus Van Valkenburg would not return to high school counseling. This was, however, with the enthusiastic endorsement of his former principal and life-long friend Michael McBride, as eventually the two of them would conceive the County's very first youth center for bullied kids, boys and girls of all ages.

Ronnie realized that the first potential causes for suicide were being initiated at much earlier stages today, with Michael readily agreeing, mostly due to the internet's various social media assaults and malevolent powers of suggestion.

Ronnie would be the main consultant and personal counselor there, recruiting his martial arts mentor Ty DeAmbrosia to create the self-defense curriculums needed for each of its various participants.

His Sifu welcomed a new direction in his particular life, too. He was tired of maintaining a dojo, with all of its business insurance, rent and liability ramifications, not to mention the parents' demands for their kids' various belt promotions, which was the way of the "entitled world" today.

Lisa would again attend college, majoring in English Literature, and try her hand at creative writing, conceiving her studio in their home, much to Ronnie's delight.

❦ ❦ ❦

Ronnie and Lisa would never see their wolves again, at least in the flesh. Both would, on occasion, dream of their divine counterparts, however, and would share with each other these reveries with enthusiasm, compassion and love.

God had ordained…

…The Conversion of Ronnie Vee was now complete.